KU-470-658

ALL WOMAN

Ray Anthony

Published by
The X Press
PO Box 25694
London, N17 6FP
Tel: 020 8801 2100
Fax: 020 8885 1322
E-mail: vibes@xpress.co.uk

© Ray Anthony 2002

The right of Ray Anthony to be identified as the author of this work has been asserted in accordance with the Copyright, Designs and Patents Act 1988.

The characters and situations in this book are entirely imaginary and bear no relation to any real person or actual happenings.   .

This book is sold subject to the condition that it shall not, by way of trade or otherwise, be lent, re-sold, hired out or otherwise circulated without the publisher's prior consent in any form of binding or cover other than that in which it is published and without a similar condition including this condition being imposed on the subsequent purchaser.

No part of this publication may be reproduced or transmitted in any form or by any means, electronic or mechanical, including photocopying, recording or any information storage or retrieval system, without either the prior permission in writing from the publisher or a license, permitting restricted copying.

Printed by Cox & Wyman Ltd, Reading, Berkshire

Distributed in UK by Turnaround Distribution
Unit 3, Olympia Trading Estate, Coburg Road, London N22 6TZ
Tel: 020 8829 3000
Fax: 020 8881 5088

ISBN 1-902934-06-7

one

They stood scowling at each other across the table, neither prepared to give an inch. All he wanted was an explanation. All he was asking was why, for the third time in as many weeks, she had seen fit to crawl in at 3am.

She owed him no such explanation. She wouldn't question him if he came in at that time. The fact that he never did was irrelevant.

This was the latest in a recent series of vehement arguments. Something was happening to their relationship. He had a pretty shrewd idea what it was. She had slowly turned off over the last month or so. At first he'd thought that he had done something to upset her. When he tried to get to the bottom of it she said that everything was fine. But it wasn't. Her behaviour had changed. They hardly spoke to each other any more. When they did, they always argued.

"Tracy, I'm only saying that if you're going to stay out late you should tell me. I'm not asking for…"

"You don't own me."

"For crissake. I sat here waiting. I didn't know where you were or if anything had happened to you."

"I am not going to give you an account of my every movement."

"I don't want an account of your every movement. A phone call would have been nice."

Her eyes narrowed as she leant across the table. "Piss off."

"Stop being so damn childish."

"Fuck off." She banged the table with her fists.

"Yes? Where would you like me to fuck off to?"

She opened her mouth as if to tell him, but instead sat back down. "This isn't working, Steven."

One of the things he had learned through bitter experience was to be cautious whenever she called him Steven.

"This relationship is not as it should be," she continued. "We're kidding ourselves. You're unhappy and so am I. This has got to stop before we end up hating each other."

"It was working."

"Yes, it was, for a couple of months. Then something happened…" Her eyes became cold, distant and calculating. "I don't love you any more," she said in quiet resignation.

"I see. Why not? What happened?" His calmness belied his true feelings.

"I don't know. I just know that I don't love you." She looked bored.

"So, you want to call it quits? Just like that?"

Looking momentarily into his eyes, she answered flatly. "Yes."

He leant back, stuck his hands into his pockets and looked around the room. "What's his name?"

She threw him one of her cutting glances. "Can't your inflated ego handle the fact that after living with you for ten months I can no longer stand the sight of you? There has to be another man, does there?"

She was aiming to hurt and humiliate him. He would be damned if he'd let her. "Don't take me for a fucking idiot."

She kissed her teeth. "You are a fucking idiot."

She wasn't going to make him lose it. He wouldn't allow her to. Taking his hands out of his pockets he folded them on the table. Then, as conversationally as he could manage, he asked, "Where's your cap?"

Her eyes went wild. "You bastard. How dare you go through my things." She jumped up, snatched her handbag off the sideboard.

He anticipated the move. He held her by the arms, yanked her back into the chair and pinned her arms to the table. She started to struggle. He let her twist and turn for a while. Unable to break free she bent to bite his hand. He leaned back and slapped her face. Her head snapped back and hair fell across her face. Like some cornered animal she stared out at him in disbelief. Whatever it was that she saw in his face frightened her.

Suddenly she pulled away and tried to kick him under the table. He heard the loud crack of shin bone against timber as her leg connected with the cross supports. The pain registered and her eyes filled with water, but she didn't make a sound. Holding her fast, he twisted the handbag out of her grasp, flicked the catch open and upended it. Make-up, keys, diary, tube of spermicidal cream and the all-important cap container scattered across the table. He released her hand.

"Who is he?"

She brushed the hair away from her face and scowled at him. With a mixture of sobs, sneers and laughter she wailed, "If you were any good... If you knew the first thing about satisfying a woman... Who is he? A real man, that's who."

He wouldn't lose it. He couldn't afford to lose it. If he did he wouldn't be able to stop himself boxing her all round the room. Clamping his mouth shut, he pushed his hands deep into his pockets. All things considered, it was the best place for them.

"I'm fed-up of your greasy fingers pawing me," she added. "Fed-up of having to say, 'I enjoyed that', when I didn't. You couldn't make my earth move even with the help of Hurricane Albert, you fucker!"

You want to know something? Size does matter. You'd do better using your finger. And another..."

The sound of woman and chair crashing to the floor made him sit up with a start. He knew what had happened, but could not explain how. One moment she was sitting opposite, her mouth opening and closing, the next she wasn't. He hadn't moved, yet his hands were no longer in his pockets.

Slowly, he stood. He looked down at her. She was lying perfectly still, spreadeagled on the floor, a bloody gash on the side of her head. He stared at her numbly; at the wholesomeness of her face, and the fullness of her breasts. Her skirt was up around her waist, a damp patch on her knickers. She was still breathing he noted. He should pick her up but he dared not, in case he ended up throttling her. Instead, he turned and without a backward glance, walked out of the small diner. On autopilot he went into the bedroom and took his rucksack from on top of the wardrobe. His mind was blank, which was just as well because if he started thinking he would go back in there and... He filled the rucksack with necessities. He stuffed a pair of trainers into the side pockets and then zipped up. Grabbing his wallet he turned to leave.

She stood blocking the bedroom door. With one hand she wiped a trickle of blood away from her ear. In the other hand she held a twelve-inch carving knife. He looked at her and the knife. She looked at him and the rucksack. They stood like that for several moments, she more frightened than he was.

"I'll come for the rest of my things later," he said finally, starting towards her.

She stood firmly in his path. "This is my flat. Give me the keys."

It was his flat in that he'd bought it and it was he who paid the mortgage. But the bad news was that it was registered in her name, on account of a CCJ from a previous life. She clearly intended to take him apart, and not just in matters of fidelity. He took the keys from his pocket and tossed them to her. This wasn't capitulation, but he had to get away from here and he had to do it now. He was on the edge of something. If he stepped over he would end up in prison.

She caught the keys and stepped backwards into the corridor. He pushed past her, went to his bicycle and started to attach the lights. He didn't fancy cycling, but that's what you get for a three-year drinking and driving ban.

She came up behind him, still brandishing the knife like it somehow protected her. He looked down at her and then heaved the rucksack over one shoulder and the bicycle over the other. She took one step closer, changed her grip on the knife and gave him a look of contempt.

"His name is Lewis... And he's white. Every time we make love, he makes me come..."

Did she really think that it meant anything to him? If the stupid cow knew anything about stabbing she wouldn't be holding the knife like she intended to butter some toast with it. Didn't she know how easy it would be for him to disarm her? Yet he did nothing, nor did he speak. Yes, she had really hurt him and the best he could manage was to suppress his desire to commit murder.

two

Denise flopped onto the bed and kicked off her shoes. Her mobile bleeped. Massaging her foot with one hand, she reached into her handbag with the other. Text message: *Gone to Dublin. Back Thursday. C u l8r. XXX HB.* No phone call. No e-mail. No explanation. Just *C u l8r. XXX HB.* Placing the phone on the pillow beside her, she eased out of her skirt then undid her blouse and wearily folded them both over the end of the bed. Taking off her bra she slid under the duvet, far too tired for anger.

***

It was 4:15 a.m. He rang the bell again, then stood there shivering, soaked to the skin. He'd left without his waterproofs and, wouldn't you know it, the heavens decided to open up.

A light finally came on and he heard footsteps coming down the hall.

"Who dat?" a gruff male voice demanded.

"Steve."

The door opened and Andy stuck his sleepy head out. Looking his visitor up and down, he laughed.

"You don't half look pitiful, like a drowned rat."

He wasn't in the mood for jokes. "I need somewhere to crash for a night."

Andy let him in. "Woman problems?"

He wasn't in the frame of mind to talk about it. "Yeah, yeah. Kinda."

Andy nodded sympathetically. "Leave the mountain here. You want something to drink?"

"Yeah, something hot, but I'll make it. You go back to sleep. I'll tell you about it tomorrow."

He didn't want to talk about it. Not now, not tomorrow, not ever.

"This is tomorrow," Andy beamed expectantly. When Steve still didn't respond he shrugged. "I'll get you a sleeping bag." With that he disappeared into the bedroom.

Andy was Steve's first, last and only resort. But the stay could only be temporary due to a certain friction between him and Katrina, Andy's girlfriend. She would allow one night of grace. Then he would have to get out, best friend or not.

"One sleeping bag, one towel… and here's a dry track suit." Andy came up behind him.

"Cheers."

"Ready to talk about it?" Andy sat, expectantly.

"It's late, I'm tired. Go back to sleep."

"I was fast asleep but I'm awake now. So, what happened?"

Steve shrugged. "It's over. That's what happened."

Andy looked doubtful. "You reckon? You'll go back. You're hooked on the woman," he said with certainty. "A mighty fine woman she is too," he added with a yankee twang.

Steve was silent. Andy got up to leave.

"The sofa's yours. See you in the morning."

"OK."

Steve had barely dozed off when he was rudely awakened by the alarm clock and something else.

"What you doin' here?" Katrina prodded him in the ribs with her bare foot.

He rolled over to see her staring down at him. Now here was another woman who could cause a whole heap of grief.

"I needed somewhere to crash for the night," he bleated softly.

"What have you said to him?"

"Nothing much. Only that I've left that bitch." He sat up and unzipped the sleeping bag.

"You've left Tracy?" She turned and headed for the door. "She's thrown you out more like."

He sighed. Here we go again.

What the hell was Katrina's problem? He could no

more jump on his best friend's girlfriend than he could one of his sisters. Maybe he'd allowed it to go too far. Maybe saying, 'we'd better stop', when Katrina was already naked was far too late. But he hadn't seen what was coming. He really hadn't. He'd only taken her out like Andy had asked him to, while Andy was in Jamaica. You don't expect your best friend's girlfriend to make moves on you, do you?

He woke up a few hours later. He climbed out of the sleeping bag, crept over to the rucksack and started rummaging around for a fresh pair of boxers. She was back, standing by the door, and he was stark bollock naked. Slowly and deliberately she pulled her dressing gown apart to give him a full frontal of the body he could have had. He froze. She kept her eyes on his cock. It was difficult for him to hide it from her. She moved her legs apart and kept that pose until he had a respectable erection. Then she smiled spitefully, wrapped the gown around her and was gone. Talk about intimidation! What did she want from him? Women the weaker sex? They didn't half know how to cause pain. He got dressed as fast as he could.

Andy bounded into the room and looked him over, "Aren't you going to wash your stinky body?"

"Late for work."

"What? Plenty of time, man. Katrina's making breakfast."

"Thanks, but I've got to split. Need to find

somewhere to live, remember?"

"I told you, you can stay here as long as you like," Andy protested.

"No offence, mate, but that sofa and me don't 'gree," he laughed.

Steve grabbed his rucksack and headed for the door, hoping that Andy hadn't noticed anything strange in his behaviour.

***

Naheed came into the workshop at about three to tell him that he had a phone call. He pulled himself from under the car and grabbed a rag to wipe his hands. With the loud music echoing around the arches, he mouthed 'thanks' and started over. She waited by the door and beamed at him.

He followed her to the office. She was waggling her arse with an exaggerated femininity. Difficult to ignore. And, of course, she was wearing a ridiculously short skirt. That was how she always dressed. Not for the first time he found himself trying to get a handle on her. She wasn't white. She wasn't black. Nor was she mixed raced. She could have been Indian except that her hair didn't look Indian. Maybe she was Mediterranean. Naheed? How old was she? About twenty-four, he guessed. Seriously criss.

She was the only woman working with seven men.

He knew for a fact that at least three of the lads had been there, including Tony the boss. Still, she was a nice girl, always smiling. And she ran the place, did everything that needed doing except fix cars.

He followed her cute arse to the phone. It was Jo. She'd got his message. "You can't go back, Steve." It took him a moment to persuade her that 'going back' was not his purpose. Eventually, she gave him the address.

He hadn't lied. This wasn't about 'going back', it was about going forward. He had to get to Fulham and give it his best shot. And, his best shots were usually good enough.

***

She had been working on it since six a.m. Finally, she managed to debug the system. She was a systems engineer, not a software engineer, this was not her bloody job! But the company's attitude was, 'We pay you a great deal of money. We're entitled to total dedication'. The software engineers had cocked up, yet again. So, yet again, she was dragged in.

Yes, they needed a fresh pair of eyes. Yes, it was just like checking your own spelling - seeing only what you expect to see. She accepted all that. But why was it always her? She wasn't in the States, Scandinavia, or the Far East that's why. She was right on the doorstep. The thing that galled her the most was that no one would say 'thanks' afterwards.

Her phone started ringing. She snatched it up on the third chime. "Denise Simmons."

"I'm really sorry, Denise. I just forgot... Denise, say something. I said I'm sorry."

"I've told you to only phone me after four."

"It's after six, you absent-minded boffin."

Turning to the clock behind her, she saw that it was 6:07. No wonder her shoulders and neck were hurting.

"Are you at home now?"

"No, I'm still in Dublin."

"We'll talk when you get home. Bye."

She slammed down the phone. They'd do a damn sight more than talk!

***

Boy meets girl; boy leaves girl; boy realises he's made a mistake and goes back to girl; girl chews up and spits out boy. 'Nuff songs had been written about the scenario. But this time it was for real.

He vaguely knew the area. The ride over had been a pain in the arse. Literally. But it hadn't taken him long to find the street. A cycle ride from Vauxhall to Fulham was more than enough time to get your argument together. However, he hadn't put one together. He was simply going to tell it like it was.

He pressed the bell for flat B. He heard someone coming down the stairs. The someone paused for a longish moment before opening the door just enough to peek out. On seeing him Denise opened it further, pulled herself up to her full height, and simply stared.

Everyone always said she was a Naomi Campbell look-a-like. It was meant to be a compliment but he felt she was prettier than Naomi. He smiled. "When you're eighteen you have some weird ideas of what's important, don't you?"

Her eyes started somewhere near his trainers and slowly worked their way up to the top of his head like they were seeing something you usually scraped off the bottom of your shoes. "What do you want?"

"You."

She did a double-take, went to shout but choked it down, then her eyes started panning to the left and right of him as if frantically seeking an interpreter for what she just heard.

"Me? You want me?" she asked sarcastically.

He gave a slight nod.

"So, you can just pack up and leave. And then after ten years without even so much as a 'Wha'appen dawg?' you drag your black backside back and park it at my door?"

"It's eight years, five months, twelve days and," he glanced at his watch, "...about four hours."

She actually smiled. "And now you want me?"

Again he gave a slight nod.

"So this has nothing to do with your woman flinging you out on the street then?"

How the fuck does she know that? Jo. How did Jo know? Brother Andy. Bastard.

"It has everything to do with it. It probably takes the trauma of something like that to make you realise that eighteen-year-old boys shouldn't go out with twenty-six-year-old women. The life experience gap is too great. An eighteen-year-old boy can't really appreciate what a twenty-six-year-old woman's got to give. When she loved him up, what she was really doing was spoiling him for other women. This morning, around seven o'clock, I clued in to this…" He did say he was going to tell it like it was.

Despite herself her eyes filled with tears, but she blinked them away.

"Also, because she was twenty-six and not eighteen she'd be more committed, because she was more committed she'd be more hurt, and because she was more hurt she'll be less forgiving." That just about completed the gist of his early morning 'revelation'. Now that he'd laid it on the line he watched closely for her reaction.

Her eyes flicked down to the floor. Without looking up she said, "I'm in a long-term relationship."

"Well, you were bound to be. But do you love him as much as you once loved me?"

Her eyes slowly came up to meet his. She didn't say anything for a while. Then she mumbled, more to herself than to him, "You can't do this."

Well, she hadn't said 'Rot in hell you bastard'. Yet he wasn't feeling elated or hopeful. Why? If this was a 'going for broke' stroke, why wasn't he feeding her some lines? He hadn't clapped eyes on her in eight years, five months, twelve days and about four hours. Why wasn't he telling her how criss she looked for a thirty-five-year-old? Why was he making it easy for her to say 'No'.

"I know I shouldn't do this. I know it's taking the piss, right? But I'm doing it because what I'm saying is real."

Her eyes flashed anger. "Did the army do that to you?"

"Do what?"

"Make you this… egotistic," she said coldly.

She probably had a point but it had little to do with the army. And much more to do with the recent appreciation of how he could be so good at getting women into bed while being so crap at keeping them as partners. If he told her that it would definitely sound like a line. "I can't change the past. All I can do is say 'sorry'."

"You didn't come round when you left the army," she murmured almost in passing, but for the first time he saw hurt in her eyes.

Her eyes went back to the rucksack for a moment then she hung her head to the side. "You can stay, but just for one night."

***

The hushed bleeping of the mobile phone woke her. Another text message: *Staying 'til tomorrow. Back late eve. XXXX H B.*

She checked the time: one o'clock. One o'clock in a hotel bar in Dublin getting smashed! She climbed out of bed and headed for the loo. Plonking herself down and rubbing the sleep out of her eyes, she had a satisfying pee and… She was having difficulty sleeping anyway and… She was seriously pissed off and… No more ands. She didn't care.

She ran a shallow bath, squatted in it and took her time, much more time than necessary for mere hygiene, washing her fanny. Then she dried herself, took some calming deep breaths, and strolled into the spare room. Already naked she slipped into the bed. He was fast asleep, lying on his side with his back to her. Placing her arm around his waist she rested the palm of her hand on the flat of his stomach, and started to stroke…

"I'm dreaming, right?"

His sleepy baritone made her freeze.

"You say you want me?"

"Ugh?" He started to turn towards her.

She used to like doing this with him. The middle of the night jump to see whether he'd wake before he got a hard-on.

"You want me? Show me that you want me." She rolled him over until he was on top of her.

"What?" He sounded disoriented, still sleepy.

Arching her back she wiggled while moving her knees under his armpits. There! She used to spend a lot of time wondering if it was just him or whether most men could screw in their sleep.

"Do you want me?"

"Yeah." Looking down at her, he still was far from being totally awake.

"Then fuck me like you want me."

In the dim light she could see his eyes blaze. She smiled up at him. No need to tell him twice. Raising himself he moved his arms until his elbows were at the back of her knees, hands under her, gripping her shoulders. Even after eight years, five months, twelve days and however many hours, she knew exactly what he was going to say next.

"Are you sure you're comfortable like this?"

"I'm comfortable, now fuck me like you really want me."

"I really want you. I really want this. And, Denise, I want you to want me too."

"I'm sure you do... Well, come on baby, here it is."

"Are you sure you're...?"

"Yes, yes, yes."

Wrapping her arms around his neck she pulled him down into a kissing embrace. Then he started to move, ever so slowly. Abruptly moving out of sync and to a different rhythm, she let him know that 'slow' wasn't what she had in mind. Breaking the kiss she breathed in his ear, "Show me how much you want me."

Now there was much more purpose and urgency about him, more vigour and masculine intensity in his every movement. Now they were really fucking, and she knew that he could easily keep this up for an hour (unless he'd changed, which she very much doubted).

The temperature under the duvet rose, with sweating skin gliding against sweating skin. She kicked the duvet away and lifted her legs over his shoulders, then kissed him to pre-empt the inevitable inquiry about her comfort. She never understood why he couldn't get it through his thick skull that she wouldn't do anything she found uncomfortable.

"Is this how much you want me? Just this much, no more?" she mocked, extending her fingers to squeeze the cheeks of his ample backside, signalling 'Faster! Harder! More!' "Oh! Show me, show me, baby. Tell me you want me."

"I want you."

"Tell me like you mean it."

"I want you."

"Fuck me like you mean it."

"Like this? Do you like it like this? Do you believe this?"

Sweat was trickling down his face onto her neck, cleavage and breasts. Now almost upright he had only one hand around her shoulder, pulling her to him in time with their synchronised bumps and grinds. He could keep this up but what she really wanted was for him to come, and come now.

"Oh Steven. Fuck me! Show me! Fuck me." Sinking her nails into his bum she drove him faster and faster. "Show me, show me, show me. Ah! Ahh! Baby, just like this! Yeah, just like thahhh… Ooh… Harder!"

He was strong, overexcited, unrestrained and with her feet somewhere near her ears, she was now bloody uncomfortable. She could feel every muscle in his body tense as fifteen stones of man pounded into her, his entire body quaking.

"Oh! Dee, Dee, Deeeeeeeeeeeee!!!"

When he gently lowered her feet off his shoulders with his cock still inside her, she made sure it popped out. Collapsing next to her he tried to kiss her fully on the lips. She presented her cheek then turned her back to him and he pulled her into a relaxed cuddle.

They lay like that, neither speaking, just the warmth of their bodies and the sound of their simultaneous breathing punctuating the silence for the next five minutes. Aroused it would only take him five minutes, unless he'd changed. Rolling onto her stomach and folding her arms under her, she raised her arse and, holding her breath, waited. Quickly sitting up, he moved to be behind her.

So predictable. After all these years and she was still able to read him. Doggy. Well, it wasn't to be. Not tonight. She stepped out of the bed and looked down at his puzzled face.

"You want me? Well, you can't have me. You had it, and now you've lost it. Forever."

Spinning on her heels she headed for the door. From the corner of her eye she had the satisfaction of seeing him punch the pillow in frustration.

three

On the plus side, going for broke lets you focus on the job in hand — no distractions, all your energies channelled into one thing. Of course, if it didn't work, the down side was all your eggs were in one basket — no alternative, no fall back position. He'd gone after the big prize with little thought about the consequence of a crash and burn; nothing in reserve. After all, it was the big prize. Because it was the big prize and a 'Yes' would mean commitment for life, he'd tried to make it easy for her to say 'No'.

What he'd overlooked was that there were ways of saying, 'No'. The world of difference between pushing someone over and taking them to the top of a skyscraper and then pushing them over. If he'd been quicker off the mark he would have seen it coming. For one thing, she was already in a relationship. She wasn't the type of woman to be unfaithful, but she was a woman. And what do women do when their men really piss them off? Sleep with other men, of course. They —

Tracy came to mind — seem to be able to go totally off a guy.

So, whoever-he-was was in the doghouse, and one man's doghouse was another man's pleasuredome.

He'd heard her moving about in the kitchen while he was in the bathroom. Ice cold. That's how he was going to be. With women, it's all about controlling anger. If you lose it, you've lost.

"Morning Steven, want some breakfast?" She greeted him with a friendly smile.

Make-up on, hair done, she was dressed in a blouse and the skirt of a business suit.

"Cheers but I've got to leave for work, thanks anyway. Can I leave my stuff here for today? I'll come by later to pick it up."

Raising a wary eyebrow she asked, "Why?"

"Saves me cycling all over the place with a heavy rucksack on my back."

"Why do you need to cycle all over the place?'"

Now it was his turn to look wary. "Flat hunting."

"Yeah, OK." Then as an afterthought she added, "You can stay here until you find somewhere. There's a spare set of keys in the bowl on the sideboard out in the hall."

What? He was sure that there was another massive skyscraper in there somewhere, but no matter how hard he stared into her eyes he just couldn't see where it was. Ice cold. "Nice. I'll catch you later."

***

He'd managed to keep a lid on it throughout the day. By the time he was leaving work he was still calm, but he knew that he wasn't anywhere near composed. Flat hunting? Why the hell should he be flat hunting? If a certain person didn't want to be reasonable then... No, he didn't want to think about what would happen if Tracy wasn't going to move her fat arse out of his flat.

This riding everywhere was getting to be a real pain. He should be making this journey in his Stag. His beautiful Triumph Stag, now there was a pleasant thought. After sorting things out with Tracy, he might go and just look it over. Yes, he'd go over to the lock-up and spend a few minutes behind the wheel. Dreaming. With the thought of his most prized possession fixed in his mind the ride didn't seem that bad.

Before he knew it, he was climbing the steps to his flat. He rang the bell. The curtains moved and he saw her staring at him. He stared back. Why didn't she open the door? She mouthed, 'Fuck off', then jerked the curtains back. He stood with his bike over his shoulder and considered this. He could simply kick the door in. After all, it was his door. No. That was not a good idea. The kicking wouldn't stop with the door. This is not healthy. If he didn't watch it, this woman was going to turn him into an axe murderer. He turned and walked down the steps.

By the time he got back to Fulham it was coming up to nine. He cycled around until he found a grocer that was open and bought a few bits. Then he went in search of a decent looking chippie. He got an extra large portion and a couple of saveloys then headed back to Denise's.

Denise asked if he'd found somewhere. He just shook his head. He was not in the mood to talk, or to listen. As soon as he finished eating, he said 'good night', had a shower then went to bed.

He woke up totally disoriented. It took several seconds to work out the unfamiliar surroundings. He rummaged around for his watch. It was 1:35. He lay there puzzled, never usually waking in the middle of the night. He heard some soft moans coming from Denise's room. He must have still been half asleep because it took him a little while to work out what they meant. Thin walls. That's the problem with these converted flats. Great!

Just what he needed, having to listen to Denise getting banged. Flinging off the duvet he jumped out of bed with some half-formed idea of busting in on them and joining in. He was already out of his room with his hand on her door before it occurred to him that he was fantasizing.

She knew he was in the next room. 'Stay as long as you like'. Hmm. Be reasonable, woman. You've chucked me off a fucking skyscraper. But it's not enough for you, right? Now, you've got to make it the Empire State Building. Quietly backing away from her door he went back to his room and threw himself on the bed. The thought that Denise could anticipate him reacting like he had was even more galling. Suddenly, he started laughing to himself. There you are giving your woman a good seeing to when, lo and behold, some geezer you don't know steps in and gives her a good seeing to. Feeling much better he got back under the duvet. Oh well, Denise was no longer his problem, she was someone else's headache now.

Problem. There was no way he was going to get back to sleep now. And of course, he now had a monster of a hard-on. He turned his mind to football. Only limited success. They were at it for at least another hour...

He woke about seven and didn't have to figure out why he hadn't had a restful sleep. It was Saturday, but he was going in to do some private work. That's one good thing about his boss, Tony, the man didn't mind if you used the garage in your own time. Having a quick shower he went to make some breakfast. He wanted to get out before they woke up. His ego wasn't up to bumping into Mr Stamina just then.

Denise shuffled into the kitchen. She was barefoot and wore a short towel dressing gown. She looked sleepy and, well, there was no other word for it, shagged.

"That smells nice." She came over to stand next to him looking down into the frying pan. "Bacon always wakes me up."

The dressing gown wasn't exactly tight around her. A fair portion of her tits were exposed. After last night he could really do without this. She smelled womanly, overpowering. He swiftly changed his thoughts to the gearbox he had to fix.

"Do you want some?" he asked.

"OK." Yawning, she rubbed her eyes, but didn't move.

He squatted down to open the fridge. That was stupid. The smell was stronger down there. He pulled out a couple of eggs and as he stood back up another shagged-looking woman walked in. This one was blonde, short spiky hair, tanned, about 5'5", heavy set and buxom with a roundish face, wearing an oversized rugby shirt. She flashed him a brief friendly smile. He hadn't smiled back, he couldn't cope with all these semi-exposed female bods this early in the morning. Especially after...

Life was so fucking unfair. There he was, right next door, while some bloke's playing twos-up with one Swedish porn star-type and one beautiful black...

It wasn't like they were holding hands or anything. They weren't even looking at each other. But there was something...

Then Denise made eye contact for the merest

nanosecond, 'You thought last night and the night before was the skyscraper? Naw. That was just me taking you up in the lift, bwoy'.

He dropped one of the eggs.

Both of them turned to look at him. Denise simply said, "This is Corrine." Then she gave him a 'Want to make an issue of it?' look. He just stood rooted to the spot, gobsmacked, and feeling really foolish. Corrine spun and opened a drawer, didn't see what she was looking for, and slammed it shut. Then she opened a cupboard and pulled out a J-cloth. She hadn't bent over far, but he'd caught a nicely shaped arse, some pubes and some snatch. And Denise had followed his eyes.

Corrine went like she was going to wipe up the egg. He snatched the J-cloth out of her hand. "It's all right, I'll do that." She had done more than enough bending over for one morning. "Why don't you have this and I'll make some more?" he managed to suggest matter-of-factly.

"I'll just have the eggs. I'm a vegetarian," Corrine informed him with a heavy 'keep your eyes off my woman' vibe.

***

"How can you say that?"

"Well she is." Andy was looking at him like he was making a fuss over nothing.

"You sure?"

Andy kissed his teeth, tapped the steering wheel, but didn't answer.

He wasn't going to leave it there. "I mean, like how long have you known?"

"What's the big deal? Come on, let's talk about something else. What's happening with Tracy?"

Tracy? He couldn't think about her. He was having enough difficulty accepting that Andy's sister Jo, someone he had known for over half his life, was a lesbian and he hadn't known about it. And that was plenty enough without adding an ex-girlfriend.

"How did you find out?"

Andy gave him a long hard stare before answering. "She came out to me. Then she told Dad and Dad told Mum," he said patiently.

"How come you didn't tell me?"

Andy looked at him peculiarly. "I thought you knew."

"How would I know? If she wasn't your sister I might have tried it on. I mean, you know I've always had a soft spot for her."

"Just as well you didn't try then, isn't it?" Nodding to himself Andy then added thoughtfully, "Let me ask you something. My eighteenth birthday party, that's when you got it together with Denise, wasn't it?"

"Yeah."

"You weren't making a play for Jo by any chance,

were you?"

"I wouldn't do that, she's your sister."

"Lie. So let me check this: at my party you make a play for my sister, who is a lesbian. But you end up with Denise, who's also a lesbian." Laughing Andy slapped the steering wheel. "Ya bitch you!"

This wasn't funny. "Did you know about Denise?"

Andy glanced in the rear-view mirror then turned to him, trying and failing to suppress a smile. "You worried?"

" 'Bout what?"

"Come on, man, this is me you're talking to. You saying that it hasn't crossed your mind that maybe lesbians are made and not born and maybe, just maybe, there was something you should've done differently?"

This wasn't funny. "No."

"Well, bwoy, you good. Coz if it was me who had corrupted, turned, a fit looking woman like that, I'd be worried."

This wasn't funny. "You haven't answered my question, did you know?"

"If I'd known I would have tipped you the wink. Anyway, according to Jo, it happened long after you." Reaching across Andy slapped him on the back. "Think, after you, no man was good enough."

This wasn't funny and this man can't have it both ways. "Jo, it's not like... she doesn't act strange or anything."

"She isn't strange," Andy said flatly.

Satisfied that he'd stop Andy skinning up his teeth, he reminded himself that this was a delicate subject. "I'm sorry, right. But Jo and Denise being dykes is a bit of a blow. OK?"

"Don't call them dykes."

Uh-uh. "You know what I mean. How do you feel about it?"

"You know what? You're homophobic. Oh, that's what they call it when you don't like 'chi chi man'. Whatever the female equivalent is, that's what you are."

"I can't help it. Denise! What a waste."

Andy lightened up. "So, your mouth dropped the same time you dropped the egg?"

"You should have been there. I didn't know where to put my face. I've got to find a place soon."

"Why?" Andy was again dead serious.

"Well you know. I can't take all this riding miles every day."

Andy's grin was back. "Wha' you ah talk 'bout? You been puffing and panting during the second half recently. Good exercise cycling, and remember it's cheap. It's not the riding that's bothering you, is it?"

"Course it is."

Andy looked at him thoughtfully then said, "She's bi…"

"By what?"

"Denise, bisexual. You could be well in. Do you want

me to find out from Jo?"

"You're a sick man. How can you even think things like that?"

"If you had both of them naked in front of you, you wouldn't be saying that."

That was such a disgusting thought. Thank God he hadn't told Andy about the midnight ambush. Thank God they were just pulling up to the flat.

"Got to split. Check you later."

"I'll find out for you," Andy grinned.

***

Okay, she could do with the rent money. But she didn't need the hassle and had only agreed to it to make a point: she wasn't threatened by Denise's past relationships, even those involving men and especially not her relationship with Steven. Denise probably didn't realise it but whenever they'd discussed her heterosexual relationships she always painted a vivid picture of what the men were like, the things they did, how they behaved, and how she felt about it. But the only one who had a name was Steven.

Now the fabled Steven needed a place to stay. OK. In fact he had stayed there the night she was away in Dublin. Corrine's suspicions were aroused. She would soon find out what he had that was so special and whether Denise still held a candle for him.

So she waited until he returned from work and
spelled out the terms: "We need to get a few things
straight. It's a month's rent in advance and a month's
deposit. The things you use, you clean. Gas, electricity
and phone are extra. How you keep your room is up to
you, the rest of the flat — spotless. No late night visitors.
In fact, I don't want strangers wandering in and out of
my home. No rolling in drunk. If you have the
occasional blow, fine, but nothing heavy, and no
cigarettes."

But he wasn't listening. There was a game on the
television.

On reflection, it should have been obvious that it
would not, could not work. She didn't need a man
perched on the edge of her sofa, wearing a leather cap
back-to-front, monopolising her television. Couldn't she
handle it? Was she fazed by his presence? Was she
threatened by him? How would she feel if he'd been one
of Denise's ex-girlfriends? Would she still feel like
saying, 'Keep your eyes off my woman'?

"On second thoughts, this isn't going to work, is it?"

Momentarily, his eyes flashed to hers, then back to
the TV. "What's not going to work…? Goal!" He was on
his feet, hopping around the room. "Two nil, two nil!
Two nil, twooo nil! Come on you Gunners!"

She gave him a moment's grace.

"You, living here."

"Referee! Off, off, off, off! Yellow? Yellow?! That's a

sending off!" he bellowed at the box.

She reached for the TV remote and switched it off.

He turned to her with incredulity, then his eyes went back to the blank screen. "It's the Cup," he said with measured restraint. "What's the matter with you?"

"If you're going to live here, we need to get a few things straight."

It seemed to take some time for her words to register. "Can't this wait 'til after the match?"

"No it can't.

"What's so important that it can't wait until after a Cup match?"

"We're gay. Providing you accept that, you can stay."

"No. I'll split. I don't need this, so I'm going. OK?" he answered with measured calmness.

She wouldn't let him off that easy.

"You can't take it can you? I suppose you think Denise should be available to you, right? Your ego can't accept that she isn't, can it?"

"Lesbian or not, you're all the fucking same. As soon as a woman thinks she has control, she starts. I've had enough crap from women to last me a long time. So, if you don't mind, I have some packing to do."

"So, you don't want to have Denise then? And us being lovers doesn't bother you?"

"What the fuck has Denise got to do with anything?

"I just want you to accept that we're gay."

"Corrine, correct me if I'm wrong, but you're the one

who is jealous, aren't you? You're scared that I might take your woman from you. She's my ex-girlfriend, same woman, hasn't changed. So she's a lesbian, same woman, hasn't changed. OK?"''

"So, you did have your eyes on my woman?"

"Eyes on your woman? You're the ones who waltz into the kitchen in the morning waving your minges in my face."

"Minge? 'Minges'? Is that another derisive description of the female genitalia? I must remember that," she smiled.

He smiled back. "You might prefer 'clout'." He switched to an effected northern accent, "As in, 't' lass had a clout like a saddle bag'." He switched back to his normal Caribbean-cum-cockney. "There's also the old favourite 'clam', as in 'bearded clam'."

"Minge? Clout? Clam?" She forced the smile to remain on her lips. "Where did you learn to speak such 'interesting' English?"

"Army."

"Of course. The army. That's when you met Denise."

"Yeah. You know, visit far off lands, meet interesting people, then kill them." He added an afterthought: "There were lotsa lesbians in the army, but they were well butch."

***

"Well, why not?" Corrine asked, struggling to sound perfectly reasonable.

Denise hated her when she was in one of these moods. She knew Corrine didn't really want him there. Corrine was only making a point, she was going to use the dinner party as a stage to flaunt her egalitarianism. She would be unbearably liberal, unthreatened, and free thinking: 'Look everyone, here's Denise's ex-boyfriend and I'm not in the least bit anxious, aren't I a truly wonderful person'. Pretentious to the point of acute embarrassment. But Denise couldn't say that, the argument would only get more heated and Corrine would make it a bigger issue than it needed to be. Pressing too hard would only arouse Corrine's suspicion and then it would only be a matter of time before she found out what had transpired between her and Steve while she was in Dublin.

"Does his being there make you uncomfortable?"

What an accusation! She saw from Corrine's expression that she didn't have to remind her to keep her voice down, he was only in the next room. "Of course not."

"Then why are you being so negative?"

"Because I don't want you to make a fool of yourself."

She slowly got up, walked over and sat in her girlfriend's lap. Putting her arms around Corrine's neck, she soothingly said, "I am not being negative. Just remember, don't drink too much."

Their closest friends, good food, a few bottles of wine... Denise didn't care whether he was there or not. No, not true. She didn't want him there at all. His presence had upset the balance in their relationship already. Her little game of making Steve suffer had backfired. She had given him a taste of what he had been missing and wanted him to beg for more. She had loved him once. Maybe still did. But he had done her wrong. He was ready to beg. She was sure of it. But Corrine was making such a big deal over him. She had been acting strange since her return from Dublin. She had left for work that morning adamant that Steve would have to go. What had happened since then to make Corrine change her mind?

four

He didn't want to spend an evening with a bunch of dykes, so he gave some lame excuse. He went out, checked a film, *Shaft Returns*. Not bad, his main man was in it, but this was the first and the last time he'd go to the cinema by himself. It was all couples. He felt like a dirty old man. He found a pub with a pool table. He let the regulars win a couple of games. He bided his time until the local Mr Big started showing off, then mannersed him. After chucking-out time he took a stroll round Parson's Green. At midnight he figured it would be safe enough to go home.

As soon as he stepped through the door Jo rushed out, took him by the arm, and marched him into the front room. "This is Steve, everybody."

As well as Jo, Denise and Corrine, there were three other women and, well, lots of glasses and lots and lots of empty wine bottles.

As far as Steve was concerned, everybody knows that dykes are butch, hairy, wear donkey jackets and monkey boots, and look like a bulldog chewing on a wasp. *Right?* After all, lesbians are women who go out with women who look like blokes, aren't they? So, a woman looking like a supermodel wasn't going to be standing there. *Right?* Well, that's not what his eyes told him. His ears were obviously still working because he got her name, Marti. She was 5'10", maybe 5'11", raven black hair in a bob, dazzling gem-blue eyes, porcelain smooth skin and the most wicked red lips. But did the agony stop there? *No.* She was also wearing a miniskirt that no woman should be allowed to wear. Legs up to her armpits and her top — it wasn't a blouse, it wasn't a T-shirt, it was a kind of see-through wrap and no bra. Oh Lord, *her tits!*

'Nuff pressure, right? When He was putting her together, He was conspicuously indulging Himself. Because he didn't stop at making a staggeringly beautiful woman. He just had to go one step further and make her horny as well. Steve's ears heard, "Babs." Babs? Oh, Babs was the woman sitting across from Marti, he hadn't even noticed her. Babs; blond, shorter, more curvaceous, beautiful as opposed to staggeringly beautiful, wearing a trouser suit. Now, if Marti wasn't there, he would have ogled Babs. No, even with Marti standing there Babs was 'criss'. It was just that Marti… look at her and you want to fuck her. Standing next to Marti, getting her glass filled, was Liz, a tallish double-criss sista wearing a short leather jacket. All she had on under it was a crossed bandelero-type leather strap. If she was wearing a garment on the lower half of her body, he didn't immediately notice. OK. He sussed the pairings, Marti and Babs, Jo and Liz. He managed a 'hello' to them.

He was losing it. He was starting to drool. *This has to be a set-up*. They were taking the piss! He stuffed his hands in his pocket. There were enough bulges on show without his input.

"Andy said you were ill." Liz was addressing him.

"Sorry?" He turned to her. Mistake. Big, big, beautiful, sad eyes.

"We should have met at our party, but you were ill," she cheerily explained.

He did have some vague recollection of an invitation to Jo's party a couple of months back. "I wasn't ill, I was lame. Busted up my leg at football. Anyway, pleased to meet you."

She rolled those big beautiful sad eyes. "You're not football crazy like Andy, are you?"

"Dunno 'bout that. We play for the same team, though."

She shifted her weight onto one foot and placed a hand on her hip, causing her jacket to open further, exposing more barely-covered tits while drawing his attention to her slender waist. His eyes tried looking in three places at the same time. Couldn't do it, so they stayed with the face. She smiled up at him, teasing. "Do you train?"

Her eyes drew him in, making him oblivious to anything else. "Sometimes."

"And you spend all your time talking about football also, no doubt."

He laughed. That was Andy all right, able to quote chapter and verse any football match ever played. "I wouldn't want to talk to you about football." That's a line. She's a lesbian. *Behave!*

Mercifully Corrine said loudly, "Come on, sit down."

He wasn't sure if that was said to them but Liz gracefully flopped into the nearest seat. As he sat next to her, Jo, still talking to Babs across the room, sat on the arm of his sofa. And just to round it off, she rested her arm across its back and sort of on his shoulders. Time to get a hold of himself and take stock of the situation.

Leaning over, Jo softly said in his ear, "They're both full-on."

Because she had spoken softly, he asked back softly. "What?"

"They're not bi. Andy said you wanted to know."

"No I didn't."

Liz turned to him grinning and equally as softly said. "Yeah, he also said that you had a crush on Jo."

"Did he?"

"Yes, he did. I thought you knew. I've been out for years, everybody knows," Jo continued in the same quiet tones.

"_Excuse me._ What are you three whispering?" Marti shouted across the room.

"Steve wanted to know whether Corrine and Denise were bi," Liz shouted back.

Good job nobody can see a black man blush.

Babs, Marti and Liz cracked up, Corrine just looked at him and Denise gave him a weak smile. Also laughing, Jo slipped her hand fully around his shoulders and nudged him playfully. Denise joining in proper then said, "I think it's really Corrine he fancies." She looked him right in the eye. "Had an eyeful you see."

He just looked back but kept his mouth shut.

"We all know straight men's favourite fantasy," Babs winked at Corrine.

He kept his mouth shut on this one as well. But Jo wasn't having any of that, she nudged him once more and said, "Take your hand out of your pocket and say something."

All six of them shrieked with laughter.

This is absurd.

Marti got up, walked all the way over to him and playfully started tugging on his pocketed arm. As she did this, her tits jiggled before his eyes. Which, of course, did not help his situation.

"All right, all right, let go." He took his hand out, crossed his legs and folded his arms in his lap.

Boy did they laugh. Jo laughed so much, she slid off

the chair arm, ending up in his lap. Marti was bent double in front of him, tits still going. Somewhere at the back of his mind he could also see the funny side of this. Just.

"I'm attracted to beautiful women, so what? Aren't you?" He tried to laugh with them.

"Have some more wine and sit down," Corrine said, calling the pack off their quarry.

Marti backed off, smiling, a certain glint in her eye. It wasn't meant to tantalise, he'd seen that very look from Katrina. This must be a woman power thing. Katrina had used it to show him what he could have had; with Marti it was what he couldn't. What did it mean? No point in causing himself brain damage trying to figure it out.

All seven of them were now sitting — on sofas, arms of sofas, and the floor — in a loose circle. He was sandwiched tightly between Jo and Liz. If he glanced left his eyes were pulled down to Liz's tits. And he didn't need to glance anywhere to see Jo's, they were right next to, and level with, his eyes. Sitting opposite him was Corrine; not good because she'd hitched up her skirt in order to sit cross-legged on the sofa and, well, he'd had enough of that in the kitchen. Next to Corrine, but on the floor, was Marti; not good because she leant forward whenever she had something to say, and she'd stretched her long, long legs, and she wasn't wearing much of a skirt to begin with, and... Oh fuck, this was not good. Babs was on the sofa over to the right; not good because every time she reached for her wineglass she aired a hormone-releasing amount of cleavage. Denise was perched on the arm of Bab's sofa, bicycle style; not good because… Jesus Christ, woman. Keep your knees together.

He sighed, it didn't matter where he looked, there was something to seriously distress his eyes.

"I can't take this."

He was on his feet. They all stopped and looked at him. He felt such a damn fool, he immediately sat back down.

"Steve, do you feel awkward?" Jo asked sensitively.

How could he answer this without making a bigger fool of himself? "No. It's… it's not that. I'd still feel this way if you were, well, normal women."

They all gave him that woman look. The look that says 'you've just said something to really piss us off', they were giving you time to think about it and then they were going to let rip. He went over what he had said. As usual, he couldn't find anything to provoke the look. No doubt he'd find out in a second or two.

"*Normal?* So, we're not normal. If we aren't normal what are we, *abnormal?*" Liz said flatly.

Was this a political correctness thing? He never did understand political correctness. He was a caveman who still believed a normal woman is one whose greatest ambition in life is to manners the dick. These weren't normal women, so what was he supposed to say? Anyway, the damage was already done. Normal or not, every caveman knows that once a woman gets it into her head that she is going to rant and rave, there's nothing you can say to stop her. Let's see now: Usual? No. Ordinary? No. Average? No. General? No. Typical? Hmm... 'I'd still feel this way if you were typical women'. No.

"I wasn't suggesting that you were abnormal..." He looked round the room at the faces glaring at him. "All I was trying to say was, it's not... the way you are... I mean... You're all dressed inna wicked style... It's disturbing me, OK?"

Jo grabbed a bottle and sloshed wine into glasses. Trying to relieve the tension? Corrine gave him an even more malicious woman look. The one that says; I'm not going to say anything more about it now; but I'm not going to forget it; I will, at some later date, and at a more appropriate time, drag it up and ram it down your throat sideways. "Try gay, much simpler," she advised.

"Dressed inna wicked style?" Mimicking a pretty good Jamaican accent, Babs teased. She, at least, seemed prepared to let the matter drop.

"I don't see why how we choose to dress should disturb you." Marti wasn't. "Were you suggesting that we shouldn't?"

Couldn't they see that, that was the whole problem?

"Enough of the outrage, let's just enjoy the evening,"

Jo decided as she sloshed more wine.

They continued yapping away, knocking back the wine like there was no tomorrow. Six drunken dykes on his hands. Could he handle it? He wasn't sure. He kept his mouth shut.

Some time later, when they were caning the liqueurs, a drunk Marti crawled over to him, exposing most of her tits, and stuck a bottle opener under his nose like a pretend microphone. "Well, Mr Heterosexual, what is your opinion on lesbian parenting?"

Lesbian parenting? Was he missing something? He hadn't really been listening to what they were saying but had been aware that they were making a lot of noise saying it.

"You mean, like two women raising a child?" He really wished that Marti, and her tits, would just get out of his line of sight. "It's all right, I suppose. But what if it's a boy? How about when he's fifteen?"

"Two loving gay parents are better than two bad heterosexual ones," Babs asserted, and in chorus they all voiced agreement.

Why don't women ever stick to the subject? "I didn't say that they weren't." Six drunken, argumentative dykes. Great. "I'm not arguing with you, you know."

"What if Corrine and Denise wanted to have a child?" Babs challenged.

"What?"

"Suppose we…" said Corrine waving her hand at

Denise "...intend to have a baby. Why shouldn't we be able to?"

"What?" Marti was now kneeling at his feet. Why didn't she just go back to where she was sitting?

"I've always planned on having a baby," Denise said at him, like it was all his fault.

"What?"

Babs snatched up a bottle, shook it vigorously with both hands — being as she preferred to drink from the furry cup she probably had no idea what that reminded a caveman of — and pointed the cork at him. "Say 'what' again! I dare you. I double dare you! Say 'what' again."

He just smiled at her . He liked her.

"It makes perfect sense that if we were going to have a child, I should be the one to have it," Corrine turned to Jo and Liz, as if seeking their support.

Denise sat up like this was news to her. "*You?* I thought we'd agreed..."

"Finance; your earnings are more than twice mine. I can work from home, you can't." Corrine finished off with a flourish in the manner of a man laying down the law to his woman.

Denise gave Corrine a 'having difficulty focusing' scan to see just how seriously to take that. Still unsure she started, "You never said. Are you sure?"

"Of course I'm sure," Corrine answered as she tried, and failed, to sit upright in the chair. "Just as I'm sure it has to be mixed race," she added like that was crucial.

Babs, Marti, Liz and Jo, reacted with a collective 'Oh yeah, fuck me, never thought of that'.

Waving her glass, Corrine added, "You know that exotic mixture of colour you get in places like Singapore?" she paused for effect then looked around the group, "but without the almond-shaped eyes."

Looking astonished Denise demanded, "Just because I'd said, you know, that that would be the only one I'd consider, are you thinking about the same one?"

"Why not?"

Open-mouthed Denise stared at Corrine then silently turned to the other women as if it was her turn to seek their support.

Women were so funny when they were smashed. He hid his mouth behind his hand.

"Well, you did say... And it has to be." Half-embarrassed, half-apologetic, Babs answered. And there seemed to be an unstated nod of agreement from the remainder.

Denise looked genuinely flabbergasted. Eventually, she managed a breathless, "OK. If you're sure."

"I'm sure," Corrine said, settling the matter.

This was the impetus for even more wine to appear. And this time the six women proved that their previous drinking had been only the warm-up. Interspersed with the occasional clinking of glasses, they must have polished off a bottle each in under fifteen minutes.

"Hmm... Tall. Say, six-two," Marti suddenly said to thin air, nodding.

"Definitely," Jo agreed. "And handsome."

"Athletic," Liz mused.

"I've got a turkey baster," Babs sniggered.

"No, syringe," Marti countered.

These four erupted with laughter. Denise, with the rigidity of someone who's drunk and trying to appear sober, addressed him somewhat formally. "Would you?"

"Would I, what?"

Corrine suddenly tensed. Liz drunkenly elbowed him in the ribs. "Consider making a donation."

"A *donation*?????"

Marti lurched up to him and the flimsy thing she had around her finally came fully open. Which raised an interesting question: if they were all dykes, how come he was the only one noticing her superb tits?

Marti grinned into his face. "Five knuckle shuffle, bashing the bishop, fifty flips, beat the meat, strangle the chicken."

He understood her allusion but couldn't see the relevance. Corrine said in a measured tone, "I don't agree with the rampant misandrists. A child's not an accessory, or a political statement. It's for the quality of life that we lovingly have to offer."

"Of course, so what are you saying?" Liz asked.

Corrine looked almost pleadingly at Denise before

answering. "Turkey baster and syringes are all manifestations of control."

Denise stared back, a dangerous inebriated look in her eyes. "Yes, *and...?*"

"I'd be appalled if I didn't know who my father was." Corrine's pleading look was still there.

"If we've learned anything in the last decade, it's that the children must know and have relationships with their natural fathers," Jo said as if this went without saying.

He could tell that there was some serious shit going down, pity he didn't understand what about.

"Yes, *and...?*" Denise's eyes remained rivetted on Corrine's.

Squirming Corrine looked down at her hands. "How would you feel if you discovered that you were conceived by a mechanical process?"

The strained, muted atmosphere suddenly exploded as everyone started to shout. Except for him that is. As the arguments and counter-arguments flew, he heard the words but didn't understand the context or meanings. Liz and Marti looked like they were shaping up to exchange blows. Denise was staring at a bottle like she giving serious consideration to hitting Corrine with it. Jo and Babs were exchanging spiteful one-liners. He just sat there, feeling like he was ODing on oestrogen.

"Well?" Denise jumped to her feet and screamed down at him.

Silence. All eyes on him. Why was he being shouted at? He looked at each in turn. "Well, what?"

"You have to have your say as well," Babs explained like he was being negligent.

All eyes were still on him, like something depended on him. Corrine was looking really worried. Why? He took a long, slow, deep breath… "I was on the platform, right? But the train left without me. Hear what I'm saying? I haven't got a clue what you are talking about?"

Now they were all looking at each other, waiting for someone else to speak.

"Come on, what's occurring?" he asked of them all.

Silence.

"Well, you don't have to tell me. But at least you've stopped arguing."

Jo overtly rested her hand on his. "Corrine and Denise would like you to be the father."

"What?" A little of the fog lifted. Did they really?

He nearly laughed, but the faces around him told him this was deadly serious. "I see. What's a turkey baster?"

"It's a… Never mind." Marti looked at him like this was some big secret.

"I'm still not a hundred percent with you."

"What about brains?" Babs threw up her hands in disgust. "What did God say after he made Adam? 'Oh fuck, I can do better than this'." They all laughed, but then Babs had to add, "He certainly said that after he made Steve."

"That was meant to be a joke, right? Want me to tell a joke?"

There was a longish pause before Corrine said, "OK, let's hear it."

"One day little Johnny goes up to his dad and says, 'Dad, what's a cunt?' After giving Johnny some earache about not using that word, his dad says, 'Your mum's asleep upstairs. Now, if you're very quiet, I'll show you'. Johnny promises so they creep upstairs and tiptoe into the room. His dad then carefully pulls back the covers and lifts up his mum's nightie. 'Now son, you see that hairy triangle', his dad whispers. 'Yes dad', he whispers back. 'Well, that's a vagina. The rest of it is a cunt'."

Denise felt it wouldn't be wise for her to defend him, instead she filled him in, slurring, "Corrine wants to conceive by sexual intercourse."

"What? Fuck me!"

There was absolute silence for about three heartbeats, then Marti said, "No. You fuck her."

Hysterical laughter from everyone except him, Corrine and Denise.

five

If this wasn't the worst hangover of her life, then it was pretty close to it. She had to run her hands along the walls to keep herself steady. Tottering into the kitchen, the sudden glare of the sun caused her to shield her eyes. Her original intention was to make brunch but she wasn't up to that. Two mugs of coffee were about her limit. She tottered back to the bedroom trying not to spill any.

Corrine was face down under the covers lying diagonally across the bed. As she placed the cups on the side, she knocked over an empty litre wine bottle. That bottle was probably the straw that broke the camel's back. She sat on the edge of the bed, moved the bottle out of the way, shook Corrine, then rested her face in her hands. God, did she have a headache.

Corrine didn't stir, so she shook her again and again. Corrine moaned, slowly rolled over and opened her eyes — she looked like death warmed up. Denise shoved a mug at her. Sitting up Corrine took it. She was about to take a sip, but instead croaked, "Don't walk around naked."

"Good morning to you too."

"I'm sorry." Corrine looked down at herself. "You're naked and I'm wearing the same clothes."

"You passed out."

"Was I that drunk?"

"Yes."

"I'm sorry."

It was difficult to concentrate. Denise took a sip from her mug. "Don't you remember anything?"

"Of course. And I meant what I said."

She wasn't in the mood for this. "You're still drunk, and I think I am as well."

"All right, so I was pissed, but I really do think I should be the one to have the child."

Denise just looked at her.

"I wouldn't have said it if I didn't mean it." Corrine had upped the volume on that and it seemed to cause her some distress because she moved her hands to her head.

"We're both too fragile to talk about this now."

"No. I want to talk about it. Don't you want to have a baby?" Corrine started to take off her blouse.

It wasn't just her head that was hurting, Denise's eyes felt like they were trying to pop out of her skull. Now was not the time to discuss this. "I know that we'd agreed to have a baby. What you said, it was sweet. I was pleased, it was a nice idea. But this is the cold light of day."

Looking as if stepping out of her skirt was beyond her, Corrine said, "Why won't you believe me?"

"Oh, does it matter?"

"Yes. "

"Corrine, I love you. But I can't see you having a baby."

"Why not?" Corrine persisted.

"Please, later, let's talk about this later." She moved further into the bed and, stretching out, pulled the duvet over her.

"Denise, this is really important. I want to have our baby."

She turned over and shut her eyes. "We are an item but are we really together?"

She felt Corrine get up and heard her walk all the way around the bed to kneel in front of her. "What do you mean?"

She opened her eyes to see a naked Corrine looking at the empty wine bottle, puzzled. So she explained. "You drank most of it then passed out."

"Why aren't we, 'together'?"

"You love your independence and, well, that and a baby aren't compatible."

All arms and legs, Corrine slipped into the bed, forcing her to move over. "I am independent because the woman I love works every hour that God sends and she is always on twenty-four hour call."

Denise suddenly asked, "Have you ever been unfaithful?"

"No. Have you?"

"No."

"Then why did you ask?"

"Be totally honest. You've never got drunk one night and maybe met someone?"

"No, never. I should be the one to ask this. You're the one who sods off to Europe for three weeks at a time."

Corrine also had a habit of disappearing for days on end without adequate discussion or explanation, but she conveniently didn't mention that. Just then, it didn't seem to matter that much. But she felt she ought to let Denise know that she didn't just suspect any more, she knew. "I don't know enough lesbians to be unfaithful."

"And I do?"

It was all in the eyes. The little glances that Denise and Steven exchanged with one another. Probably didn't even realize they were doing it. But Corrine knew, those glances spoke a thousand infidelities.

"Well, don't you?"

Corrine slowly sank into the pillow and stared at the ceiling. Denise's head wasn't really up to this. Why was Corrine pushing it?

"Do you love me?" Corrine continued, still staring at the ceiling.

"Yes. Of course I do."

"I love you so much I let you do what you want."

"I love you. I adore you. I want to be with you forever. I want us to be closer. That's why I want to have the baby."

Something wasn't adding up, but Denise needed a clear head to figure it out.

Corrine slowly slipped her hand around her.

"Get off!" How could she even think of that now? "Sorry. I'm tired. Let's get some sleep. I adore you too."

She had just closed her eyes and was about to drift off when Corrine gently shook her. "Baby?"

"Yes."

"I was also serious about what I said about him being the father. It means a lot to me, because he means a lot to you. I also meant what I said about the method. You understand, don't you?"

Denise understood that there was more to this than met the eye. "I don't agree. I don't like it. But, I'll accept it and I'll try to understand."

"I…"

"I said I'll try to understand. Now sleep!"

Corrine was smiling at her. "Our baby matters. I woke up with that thought and didn't want to go back to sleep without it." She shrugged. "I'm doing it for you. It's my sacrifice to you. Because you've always said that he's the only man you'd want as a natural father."

Denise opened her eyes and smiled. "Bet you don't remember telling Steven to show you his cock last night."

Corrine put her hands over her mouth. "Oh my God! I didn't."

"Yes you did. You were legless. Weren't we all."

"Did he?"

"No, he just laughed and said he didn't want to frighten you."

"This is awful, I don't remember." Corrine looked mortified.

"He was all right about it. He can be really funny when he loosens up…"

* * *

Corrine was still out for the count as Denise shuffled to the kitchen in her dressing gown.

Her pounding head needed food. As she peered into the fridge, she saw Steven standing by the kitchen door smiling at her. He closed his eyes and shook his head. It was so difficult to break the habit. She'd done as Corrine asked, she wasn't naked. But she hadn't bothered doing up the dressing gown. She was far too hung over to be embarrassed and, anyway, it wasn't anything he hadn't seen before. She picked some eggs out of the fridge and adjusted the dressing gown.

He strolled over to her. "I tell you what. Why don't you take a seat, and I'll make an omelette?"

Now that he was closer to her she noticed that he

smelled of soap and beer. "No, it's OK."

"Omelettes are my speciality." He took the eggs out of her hands. "Now sit."

As she backed into a chair and sank into it, she noticed that the kitchen was spotless. Everything was washed and cleared away. "Have you been up long?"

"Had a match, we won three-two, then a few beers."

How could he look so fresh after last night? "What's the time?"

"Half-four. Does Corrine want some as well?"

"Yes, she does."

"OK. Two omelettes coming up."

He started whistling tunelessly so she rested her head on the table. It was probably a good idea to close her eyes.

"You know you're going to have an AIDS test."

She opened her eyes to see Steven turning to face Corrine who was standing by the door. Steven was trying not to laugh; Corrine was wearing only a vest; hairy triangle on full view and breasts almost hanging out. He shook his head, smiled to himself and turned back to the cooker. She thought she heard him mutter, 'Unreal'. Smiling he turned back to face them. "Why don't we all sit?"

After serving up, he placed the frying pan in the sink then sat between them. Denise looked down at her plate. A spaghetti omelette — novel. She tasted it, not bad. In fact, it was pretty good. There was garlic, butter and black pepper in this. She looked at him appreciatively.

"I told you it was my speciality." He winked then turned to Corrine trying to get the measure of her without gaping at her chest. "Are you still pissed?"

"No, certainly not."

"Oh, I see," he mused unconvinced.

Denise felt conflicting emotions. There were some things she desperately wanted to say to Corrine. But not with Steven there. There were some things she ought to say to Steven. But not with Corrine there. Did they have things to say to each other in her absence? She wasn't sure if, in her heart of hearts, she could face up to the proposition and its ramifications. Yet there the three of them sat, playing out the drama.

He folded his arms and leaning forward looked each of them in the eye in turn. "Look, let's take this nice and easy, for my benefit, right? Last night a lot of things were said. I'm not too sure what was meant and what wasn't. Know what I mean?"

"No." Corrine answered flatly.

He slowly rocked from side to side in his chair. "Last night was funny. I don't mean funny. It was fun, like, really interesting. I should have been taking notes. Do you two remember what happened?" He looked up at them in wonderment. "I mean *everything* that happened. You lot were fucking outrageous. I used to be in the army, right, but I ain't never seen anything like that.

This morning I woke up and thought, 'Fuck. I've been to a lesbian wife-swapping party or something'. I ain't a prude or nothing but you guys were talking about doing things I'd never even thought of doing to a woman. And when, what's her name... Babs, was talking about something and I said, 'I don't know what you mean', what did she come back with? 'I'll show you'. Before I could say 'Wha'ppen Jack Rabbit?' Liz had peeled off her clothes so I could have a demonstration. Do you remember any of this?" He started to laugh. "No need to get stressed about it. It was a wild and interesting night. Talk about how the other half live."

Denise shrugged. "What else happened?"

He tittered some more. "You don't remember, do you? Are you sure you want to know?"

The damage was already done. "Yes."

"Well, I'm now up to speed on the finer points of vibrators. No puns intended. Well, each to his own."

"Don't be patronising," Corrine attacked.

He looked at her sideways. "I wasn't being patronising. I wasn't being anything."

Denise felt she should head off any further verbal assault. "We also need to know about your family's medical history. We need to know about things like cases of sickle-cell anaemia." She tried to sound business-like.

He turned to look at her sideways, curious. "Oh,

yeah?"

"Yes, of course," Corrine snapped.

He tapped his fingertips on the edge of the table. "I don't want to get into a bust-up here. But... I mean... Seriously... You two just, you know... Whole heap of things were said last night and that's cool. But today is today, so..." He continued tapping. "There are two things here, right? First, I don't think you two are serious. You could say that's none of my business. And second, I don't want to get involved in something like this."

"This is your moment of power, isn't it? Your chance to withhold from the dykes. And to punish Denise," Corrine retorted with what Denise considered an exaggeration, whether there was a nugget of accurate perception there or not.

He rubbed his temple like he had a headache. "Oh, this is silly. I'm not withholding, I'm just saying what I feel. No, is the answer."

"Why not?" Corrine asked, looking as hurt as Denise had ever seen her.

"I'm really trying here. This has got nothing to do with you being lesbians. If a spar came up to me and said, 'Look, I ain't got no seed, I want pickney, deal with my woman for me'. I'd still say no."

Denise understood that he had given this some consideration. "This hypothetical spar. Why wouldn't you?"

"I wouldn't want to sleep with somebody else's woman. That just leads to problems."

Corrine pulled her hand away then stared questioningly into his eyes. "Have you been in this situation before?"

"No."

"Is it to do with your girlfriend?"

"No. It ain't got nothing to do with nothing. I just don't think it should happen."

"Steve, please try and understand this," Corrine said calmly, seriously. "A woman doesn't stop being 'all woman' because she doesn't fancy men. Nor does her maternal instincts, biological clocks, etc, shut off because she's sucking pussy. I have as much desire to have sex with you as you have to sleep with another man. But I want this child. Denise wants it. Do it for her."

He lowered his head in exasperation. "I understand that. There was a time when... well, I used to think that all you had to do was get me a naked woman and I'd fuck her brains out. I'm starting to see that there's more to it than that. I can't explain it, but I know I'll regret it."

Denise asked hopefully, "What about just a donation, would that matter? I mean, if you didn't have to sleep with anyone."

"Do you mean in this situation or the spar situation?"

"Either."

He cocked his head and stared at the ceiling thoughtfully. "Still tricky." He turned to Corrine. "How do you expect me to have sex with a woman who has as much desire to have sex with me as I have to sleep with another man?"

Corrine tried to find a compromise. "If Denise... were with us... would... would that be more... interesting?"

Denise looked at Corrine like she had completely lost her mind. Before she could speak Corrine continued. "You're turned on by her. I'm turned on by her. If she's there, we wouldn't have a problem," she said, trying to sound lighthearted. "I'm simply floating an idea. If Denise was part of the package, that might help." She didn't sound convincing even to herself."

Steven shot to his feet and glared down at Corrine. "Right, 'nuff. Done." He kicked his chair back and headed for the door.

"Steve, please. "Corrine, we need to talk." Denise found that her hand had formed into a fist wanting to sock Corrine between the eyes. Steve stopped at the doorway and turned to face them, grinning.

"All right, let's say you are me. You are approached by two women who want you to father their child. You're diplomatically trying to say no, then one of them comes out with, 'You can have both of us'. How would you react? I've only got three GCSE's but one of them is chemistry. I know what a catalyst is and I don't want to be one." He grinned some more, turned and sauntered out.

Blocking the blow, Corrine caught Denise's arm and easily pinned it to the table. Staring coldly back at her, she demanded, "Do you want this baby or not?"

six

"Let me pull over, so that I can slap you without causing an accident."

"What?"

"Better get your arse in gear and get her pregnant then."

"What?!"

"Never say no to pussy when it's on offer."

Andy used to have the morals of a tomcat. Katrina put a stop to that. Well, at least he behaved when she was around. "I think it's a reasonable request," Andy added casually.

"So you'd do it?"

"I don't understand all this fuss. You're sitting in my car complaining that the woman wants seeding. Not only that, but she doesn't mind if Denise plays as well. Am I hearing right?"

"I'm not complaining. I'm just saying it's weird."

Andy snorted. "Weird? Is she ruff? Is her face grim? Is she nasty and 'orrible?"

"No, not really, she's OK."

"Then there's only one question here: what the fuck are you waiting for?"

That was more like the Andy of old. The pre-Katrina Andy. Caveman Andy.

"I've got it! No tits, right?"

"What?" He hadn't really been paying attention.

"Don't deny it. You are definitely a tits man. She's deficient in the tits department, that's why you're not interested."

"Nothing wrong with her tits," he answered defensively and sought some way to change the subject.

The bass was kicking Andy didn't seem to mind trying to have a conversation with the boom box pumping.

"You haven't forgotten what happened at Catterick, have you?"

"Catterick? What's Catterick Garrison got to do with anything?"

"That club in Richmond, gal took you round the back, remember that?"

He saw what Andy was getting at. He should've known better than to tell him about what Corrine had said. "That gal was well was pissed."

"What did you do?" Andy asked in mock disapproval.

"She could hardly stand."

"Yeah, but what did you do?"

"You know what I did. I put her in a taxi and gave the driver a tenner."

"Gal grabs you, takes you round the back for the business, and you put her in a taxi?" Andy mocked.

"She couldn't have been more than sixteen."

"So what?" Andy started to laugh. "What happens the next morning? Warning order; inna Hercules; deployment; don't clap eyes on a woman for the next three months... That should have taught you one lesson - stop being inwardly intelligent!"

"Would you be saying that if it was Jo?"

"She wouldn't fucking ask you, 'nuff man after her."

"Yeah, but say she had."

"Look star, the same principle applies. A woman is a woman is a woman. Deal with it."

"Just like that?"

"Yeah, just like that. Stick to the four F's and you can't go wrong. Find, finger, fuck and forget. Same thing."

"No it's not. This is completely different."

Andy turned to him and smiled. "Count how many women you've shagged then fucked off, never to be seen again."

He couldn't count. "We're not in the army now, mate."

"Same thing."

"Don't talk such foolishness." He should never have told Andy about this.

"Foolish? The only foolishness is coming from you. Woman wants you to fuck her till she gets pregnant and you're whining about it?"

He looked at Andy but didn't speak. No point in continuing the conversation. This topic was one of Andy's many blind spots. Fortunately he didn't have that defect. If he had, he'd have fucked Katrina, and not lost any sleep over it. How would Andy have liked those onions?

"Just deal with her, OK?" Andy pulled up outside the house.

He ignored that and opened the door. "I'll hook up with you Thursday." He got his bag out of the boot and headed for the gate.

"Steve! Nike!"

He turned around. *Nike?*

"Just do it." Andy gave him a broad grin then laid down rubber as he and his BMW took off.

He watched him take the corner without slowing then heard the engine whine as the turbo kicked in, bass still pumping. A highly tuned, rechipped, souped-up car — all his own handiwork. He laughed to himself as he opened the door.

At the top of the stairs there were a couple of suitcases. He looked them over then figured that was none of his business. He dropped his bag in his room and went into the kitchen.

A woman was sitting on the edge of the table with

her back to him. She was leaning out the back window smoking a cigarette. She turned to look over her shoulder at him. It was Babs. She pulled in her head and quietly said, "You know what these ex-smokers are like."

He wasn't sure what she was talking about but nodded. She slid around the edge of the table to face him. She looked different without make-up, but still sexy as she tossed the cigarette out the window.

"I'm only stopping for a couple of days, until I sort myself out," she said like it was necessary to explain.

He shrugged. "I was gonna make a coffee, do you want one?"

"Please." She fidgeted with her hands then looked at the floor before looking back at him and saying, "Corrine will only be about an hour. Denise has gone up to Newcastle for a couple of days…"

"Oh, I see." Why was she telling him this?

She took out another cigarette, lit it, took a couple of puffs then went to over to the window. She didn't seem to know what to do with herself. Noticing him staring, she said, "I don't normally smoke."

"Right… Do you normally take sugar?"

She shook her head and vacantly stared out of the window. After a little while she asked, "Corrine said it was OK, but do you think Denise will be bothered by me staying? I mean, I don't want to cause any problems."

"Why would it cause a problem?"

"When you get yourself a reputation..." she trailed off as if talking to herself.

"What kind of reputation?"

She turned and looked him in the eye. "A reputation for stealing other people's girlfriends."

He was going to laugh but thought better of it. "And do you?"

She must have seen something in his face because she seemed annoyed. "You were there, you saw what happened."

"Have you and Marti had a bust-up?"

For a second she looked like she was going to burst into tears. "Liz and Jo, Marti and me. And it's all supposed to be my fault."

"You mean you aren't all into free love and now there are repercussions?"

"When I got back, I found my clothes cut to shreds on the doorstep."

Maybe life wasn't that different on the other side of the tracks. "So where have you been for the last three days?"

She just shrugged.

"There is something I don't understand here. Like, when it started, nobody was looking like they minded."

She peered into his eyes as if searching for something. "I don't remember how it started. All I remember was waking up next to Liz. God it was scary.

I got home as quickly as I could."

No. Life wasn't that different on the other side of the tracks, after all. He suppressed a smile. "Well, *I* remember."

"Do you?" She sounded desperate and disbelieving at the same time.

"Yes I do. I don't know who started it, but you were snogging Liz. You weren't exactly being subtle either. Everybody saw what was going down. Nobody said anything. I thought…"

"Are you absolutely sure?"

"Sure, I'm sure."

"That bitch." She slammed down her mug.

"What?"

"I'm never going back to her. "Spiteful cow. I didn't burn all her dresses."

"I'm obviously missing something here. What are you talking about?"

"One night she went off with someone," she explained. "I took a couple of her dresses into the garden and burnt them."

She sounded as if her actions were perfectly reasonable. He pondered that for a while. What would a man do in that situation? Leave, throw her out, beat up the other party, maybe even beat her up. He'd never think to burn her best dress, would he? He now saw that he had missed a golden opportunity with Tracy. "And you think she's getting you back?"

"She hacked my best clothes and dumped them on the step."

"But you also went off with someone else." He shrugged.

"We didn't have sex. We might have caressed each other but I know we didn't. I'm sure that we didn't."

She looked embarrassed but sounded definite. Interesting. He wondered whether the Marti and Jo pairing was also a non-event.

"I wish I'd considered this earlier. Then I wouldn't have sent Corrine to see her. I should make her beg me to come back." She had a seriously vindictive look in her eyes.

"Corrine has gone to see Marti?"

"I thought… We've been together for over three years, nearly four."

"Right."

She took a couple more puffs of her cigarette and flicked it out the window. "Corrine said that you're having second thoughts about you-know-what."

"I'm not having second thoughts. I don't want to do it."

"But didn't you say you would do it for Denise?"

"Yeah, but I don't think she will agree to me doing you-know-what with Corrine."

"She will." Babs seemed positive.

"Yeah? What makes you so sure?"

She stared at him for a bit. "She would, with you."

Then she shrugged. "The child has to be mixed-race and you aren't a complete stranger. A rather elegant resolution, wouldn't you say?"

That was really fucked-up reasoning, but he wasn't going to argue. "I still don't want to."

Something occurred to him. "Is this sort of thing common?"

"I have a six-year-old daughter."

"Really. Where is she?"

She looked him up and down like the Babs of old. "With her father of course."

"Oh."

"Not a donation. I'm divorced. But I've always been a lesbian." Her knowing smile had changed to a teasing one.

"I hope you don't mind me saying so, but this is definitely weird."

"Nothing weird about it. He was a Brazilian, of uncertain orientation, who wanted to stay in the country. We got married, lived together, but Her Majesty's Immigration Service was still not convinced. So, I became pregnant." She saw him opening his mouth. "He is rather wealthy and we did sleep in the same bed."

This was just the sort of mercenary attitude that pissed him off. "What about the kid?"

"Carlotta is fine. We both love her dearly."

He turned to leave the kitchen. "This is just too

bohemian for me."

"Whatever. I think you should do it. It would make both Corrine and Denise very happy."

He glanced back. "It wouldn't make me happy."

"Steve, think about it. What more can a woman offer than to have your child?"

"It wouldn't be my child," he replied, stepping out the door.

* * *

She knew from bitter experience never to get caught in the middle of a domestic row. But somehow she felt partially responsible. Added to that, Babs and Marti were her closest friends. She wasn't interested in the details, yet for friendship's sake she thought she ought to get them together. After that it would be up to them.

It hadn't taken much persuasion to get Marti to come. All she'd done was to find out what happened with Jo — very drunk sex could hardly be called sex — then point out the obvious; Babs and Liz had got up to no more, no less, than that. Corrine already knew that Jo and Liz had agreed to disregard that night. Marti, however, wasn't ready to forgive and be forgiven. She wanted reconciliation but with strings attached. Corrine strongly suspected that this was because Marti was seeing another woman. Added to that, she and Jo had occasionally 'comforted' each other. Mind you, that was before either Denise or Liz was on the scene. The chances were that Liz knew about it, but this was something Denise could never find out.

As she followed Marti into the front room, a rejuvenated Babs flew out of the kitchen to confront them. Holding up her hands for silence, Corrine backed out, pointedly closing the door behind her. The shouting started before she reached her bedroom door.

She tried to ignore the escalating argument by reading. Easier said than done. That was her furniture they were throwing around. Then the deep male voice imposed itself over the clamour. Tossing her book aside, she dashed back to the front room.

Like a terrified mouse caught between two fighting cats, a topless Steve had them by the fronts of their blouses, prising them apart, each woman trying to get to the other. He seemed to be getting the worst of everything.

Marti lunged, knocked Steve into Babs, and all three crashed down on the sofa which toppled back. For a moment there were three pairs of legs in the air. Marti's head bobbed up, she looked round wildly, then started raining down blows. Steve was still sandwiched between them.

"Stop. Or get the fuck out of my house," Corrine cried out.

The combatants got to their feet and guiltily looked at the upturned table, but not each other. Wide-eyed,

Steve lay on the floor. There were deep scratches on his face, neck and shoulders. Blood seeped out.

Apart from being red in the face and somewhat dishevelled, neither Marti nor Babs had a mark on them. They were more concerned with possible broken fingernails than with any damage they'd done. Eventually Steve got to his feet and staggered out wordlessly.

"Get your things," Marti ordered.

Babs had her moment of token defiance then turned to Corrine, "Sorry about this." Then fluffing her hair, she sidled out.

"Yes, sorry," Marti said in a tone which was anything but apologetic.

Corrine bit her tongue.

***

He always left his clothes on the floor so that, if necessary, he could find them and get dressed quickly. Some lessons he'd learned the hard way — hangars were a chick issue. He had stripped down to his pants and was sitting on the bed. He was scratched to buggery and his was the type of skin that scarred easily. He should have been angry, very angry. But the sensation of two handfuls of rowdy, sweaty, snarling, women was sort of...

There was a knock at the door. Before he could open

his mouth, Corrine stuck her head in. When she saw his state of undress she hesitated for an instant, then bold as brass, breezed in.

She had a bottle of Dettol and some cotton balls in her hand. Without so much as a 'by your leave', she plonked herself down beside him. Still without speaking, she soaked a cotton ball in the Dettol and diligently started to daub his face. It stung like hell but he sat there impassively.

"They've gone," she said as she worked down from face to neck. "I've been to the doctor's."

He figured that she wasn't just making conversation, which meant this had some relevance. "Yeah?"

"Yes. She's given me the chart. Now, all I have to do is take my temperature in the mornings."

"I see." He didn't. This had gone far enough and he was about to tell her so.

"It'll be about the middle of next month," she said matter-of-factly.

"Right."

"I know it's… it's an imposition, but after the test, we'd feel more comfortable if you didn't have sex with anyone until I conceive."

He'd wait until she was finished before giving her a piece of the sharper side of his tongue. When she did look at him, her eyes blazed with determination. She was forcing herself to do something she abhorred. This he understood perfectly. He'd been there, seen it, done it — rock climbing, Wales, middle of winter. He'd have preferred to be anywhere except clinging to the side of a mountain, soaked to the skin, freezing his balls off, with no feeling in his fingers. But that was the army, you simply couldn't say, 'I ain't gonna do it'. He thought about modifying his approach. As he opened his mouth to tactfully tell her where to get off, she lent over to him and before he realised what she intended, kissed him. No, it wasn't a kiss. It was a lip press. He didn't feel awkward, he wasn't embarrassed, just surprised. And of course, he didn't respond. Instead of backing off, which he'd expected, she kissed him again. This time, eyes closed, trying to get some umph behind it. He did his best not to smile.

In the manner of someone thinking, 'that wasn't as bad as I thought it was going to be', she asked, "Will... will you shave... before?"

He took a deep breath. "Corrine, I have to say this... I admire you and what you are trying to do. But I'm not the guy."

Her hurt expression told him that she had misunderstood. "Do you have any condoms?"

The question threw him. "What? No. Why did you ask that?"

"If you had one," she said, looking into his eyes, "I'd show you right now that I'm still all woman."

He held back an urge to laugh. "Condom? I thought you wanted to get pregnant."

She stood. "It will take about two weeks to get the result if you have an AIDS test on the National Health. But if it's private, you get it the following day." She pushed her glasses further up her nose. "I suppose it's only fair that I pay."

"Have you ever slept with a man?"

"No."

"You don't know much about men, do you?"

"So?"

"I mean, how do you know you're a lesbian if…"

"How do you know you're heterosexual if you've never slept with another man?"

"Don't get stressed, I'm only trying to understand, OK? I suppose that this must feel a bit like taking medicine," he continued trying to be conciliatory.

"Medicine?"

"You know, get it down your neck in one gulp. So that the unpleasantness is over and done."

She almost smiled.

"Look, I'm still not sure that you getting pregnant is such a good idea. But, I can see that you're really committed to it. So why don't you spare yourself the hassle. I'll do the donation bit." Now he'd said it, he felt he was being damn generous.

Looking well vexed she said, "I've already explained. I don't want to do that. I want the conception to be natural. I just believe it's right."

"That's the bit I can't get my brain round. Is this a

religious thing?"

She looked at him as though he was insane. "No."

"All right, don't go off the deep end here, but is it to do with you wanting to break your duck?"

The look was still there. "Break my duck?"

"Yeah, I know you're gay, right, but is it because you want to lose your virginity."

Her face cracked into a grin. "I've been sexually active since I was seventeen. I have never slept with a man because I never wanted to." She gave him a genteel smile. "Why don't you look on it as a challenge?"

"Normally I like challenges but this is a lot more than just a challenge. It's a head-fuck, for me at any rate. Look, and don't get angry, in my head I know that Denise is a lesbian, right? But in my heart, I ain't there yet. Plus you aren't just any lesbian, you're her girlfriend. Get me?"

She clasped his hand and smiled. "You're really quite sweet, aren't you?"

That smile told him he'd just made the situation much worse. Up to that moment it had been, 'nothing personal, just business'. Now she looked as if she'd decided that he was an OK human being. He couldn't see a way out, so he smiled back. "Men usually interpret women calling them sweet, as 'you're a nice bloke, but I won't sleep with you'."

seven

Denise had only been away five days. In those five days the baby situation had progressed to an alarming extent. Corrine had visited the doctors and Steve had already had his AIDS test. No one had consulted her. She knew she needed time to adjust to the idea of Corrine having the baby, not to mention Steve fucking her. But how to broach the subject? Answer: as soon as possible, in the front room, the straight-to-the-point way.

"Steven, do you mind if I ask how many women you've slept with since… you know, me?" she casually asked.

"What if I mind? You've asked now."

"Do you?"

"Mind?"

"Yes."

"Depends on why you want to know."

"I just wondered," she kept her tone conversational.

"Why?"

"You do realise it will take a very special man to

sleep with Corrine."

"Why would it?"

"It's obvious," she smiled at him.

"Is it?" His expression was deadpan.

Clearly she was going to have to coax it out of him. "Of course, you know she has no experience with men. Therefore, you'll need to be, shall we say, very understanding."

Leaning against the door frame and folding his arms, he smirked. "You saying I wasn't understanding enough with you?"

"You were only eighteen and I was…"

"Yeah, I remember, a twenty-six-year-old virgin. Not impossible, but unlikely. Makes perfect sense now."

She winced. "I was a virgin at twenty-six because I was going to keep my legs together until I met a man worth opening them for."

Blinking slowly he said, "Sorry for saying that. And for letting you down."

It wasn't easy for her to forgive him for that. She'd waited and waited and waited until the day when she could make him pay. Now the time had come, she no longer seemed that interested in revenge. "You didn't let me down," she told him. "You were still growing up."

"Can I ask you something?" She nodded so he continued. "Have you slept with other men?"

Taken aback she hesitated then said, "Is that

relevant?"

"Yes."

"Why do you want to know?"

"Just answer the question."

Unflinchingly she stared up at him. "Yes, I have."

"Many?"

"Enough. Why do you want to know?"

He tittered then said, "If you don't want me to sleep with Corrine, then just say so."

"Did I say that?" She was starting to get annoyed.

"No. But I think you don't want me to and you know enough about me to try and fuck with my head."

Was she that transparent? "Don't be ridiculous. I love her, I want to be sure that you'll be considerate, that's all."

"Because you know some of us aren't very considerate, right?" Unfolding his arms he stepped past her and headed for the stairs. "Is that why you're a lesbian?"

Turning, she quickly caught up with him. "No. I…"

"Look Denise, I don't know how many times I have to say it, I don't want to do it. But Corrine is totally determined. If you want it to stop, talk to her."

She followed him downstairs. "I don't want it to stop. We both want a child. I thought you understood that."

He bounded out the door, through the gate then suddenly stopped and turned to face her. She more or less ran into him. He grabbed her instinctively around her waist. As soon as she was steady, his hand dropped to his side. The usual awkwardness returned with more than usual intensity.

"I know you're not a man, right? But the principles must be the same. Now, if I had a woman and some circumstance turned up where she had to sleep with another man, right, no matter what I said, no matter what I agreed, it wouldn't be OK. So, just stop being a smart arse and say what's on your mind. If you ain't happy about it, you gotta say so."

"I'll be happy once I know you'll be considerate."

"All right, I'll be considerate. Happy now?"

"All three of us are in a strange situation, all under the same roof. The only way this is going to happen is if everybody is open and honest."

"Tell me 'bout it. Just think, the army saved us."

"You what?"

"Suppose we'd got married or something, then one day you'd come to me and say, 'Stevie bwoy, you just ain't doing it for me'."

"I suppose so."

"Good... Denise, how you feel about this bothers me. You haven't told me."

While she hadn't got to the bottom of her misgivings, she felt that she'd inadvertently cleared the air between them. "I desperately want this baby," she half lied.

He assessed her for a moment. "All right. If you're

OK about it and OK about me and Corrine, then fine."

She hesitated before phrasing her next question. "What about, you know, what Corrine…"

"You mean the 'just the three of us' scenario?" Then he simply roared with laughter.

***

" 'Nuff man ah beg for this," Andy said, rocking in his driver's seat with sarcastic laughter. "You have it inna your lap and you turn it down?"

He hadn't said a word to Andy about it. He wasn't going to say a word to Andy about it. Yet Andy knew everything about it. It had filtered out to Jo who had passed on all the intimate details. Some women love chat too much.

"Come on, Steve, you have to talk. Two women. Both criss. And you pass it up. Wha; ah gwan?"

"You forgetting that they're lesbians?" he said sullenly.

"Jesus, man, just think what you could do. I mean, like, anything."

He turned to Andy. "What are you talking about?"

Turning to him, Andy almost drove into the back of the car in front. "Think. Two lesbians doing the business, you join the party. Fuck man, I'd kill for that."

He saw what Andy was getting at — he'd seen 'nuff videos. But whenever he applied twos-up thoughts to himself, he'd always made love to one woman and then the other. And he'd never met women who would even do that. He formed a mental picture of Corrine and Denise making love to him together. He couldn't see what Andy was getting so hot and bothered about. "It ain't like I met them in a club or anything. We all live in the same house and Denise is…"

"That's what I mean." Andy banged the steering wheel in exasperation. "It doesn't get any better than that." He was moodily silent for a bit then perked-up. "Well, at least it isn't too late."

"What?"

"You've got your foot under the table, innit. You can still turn it round."

"What?"

Snapping his head angrily round at him, Andy barked, "Do you want me to draw you a map. Make some moves, float the idea, test the water. You've still got, what, two/three weeks?"

Steve remembered reading something about the dangers of parents who live out their ambitions through their children. Now, just because Andy was shacked-up with a slag but didn't know it, he wasn't going to live out his sexual ambitions for him. But he might as well find out what he wanted him to do. "You mean, like, just ask them?"

"No, dickhead, be subtle. Say you've been thinking about what the other one…"

"Corrine."

"...said. And you think she might be right, coz you're feeling heaps of stress, or something like that."

Keeping appropriately silent for a reasonable length of time, he then said, "That would be like saying, I ain't interested in Corrine."

"Don't be a damn fool. I said, be subtle. She was the one who suggested it in the first place, right? All you have to do is play on that."

In one sense he was very annoyed that they'd told Jo about this. She, and through her Andy, had taken it as read that he would go through with it because his dick couldn't be tamed. Infact, he was going along with it because he couldn't see a polite way out. But there was bound to be a hop-off point before the actual deed needed doing. In another sense, it was kinda fascinating to see Andy worked-up like this. They'd been pals since primary school. Served in the army together. Saw action together. Chased women together. But he had never known Andy was kinky. Until now.

Back when Andy was in Jamaica, Katrina making moves had jokingly said something about wanting him to tie her to a bed. Not really listening to what was being said, he'd jokingly answered that he couldn't see the point of doing anything with a woman who couldn't move. If he had been really listening, he would have seen what was coming and perhaps sussed that she and Andy were into some strange shit. That was his problem, wasn't it — not listening to women. In retrospect, Katrina slamming the door shut and stripping off shouldn't have been a bolt out of the blue. There had been a playful, overt and long lead-up. He'd walked into it because he thought of her as a mate and he never expected his best friend's girlfriend to move on him. But by then it was much too late to say 'no'.

Had he ever really listened to Tracy? And would things have worked out differently if he had? It wasn't really up for discussion. It was water under the bridge. Almost.

"I want to know what's going on in that head of yours." Smiling, Andy elbowed him and winked.

No, you don't. "Right, I see. And if they bite?"

"Then you got to say you don't want to upset any apple carts, ain't yah?" Andy answered like that should have been obvious.

"Boss, me nuh understan'?"

Warming to the task, Andy eagerly explained. "Like, you know, you tell them you want everything relaxed. So, they just do what they normally do and you'll join in. See it deh?"

At this point he almost burst out laughing. Barely managing to control it he kept a thoughtful expression. "Yeah. Sweet."

"Fucking hell, man. If you pull this off, I want all the details. Everything."

"Sure." If he'd said any more, he would have cracked

up.

All of a sudden, Andy started looking worried. "I know you, right. Be subtle, don't fuck it up."

"Wicked."

"Radical."

They touched fists.

***

Before they always had fun doing things together. Now that they were 'together', doing nothing together was just as much fun.

Corrine knew that she'd taken too much baggage from her last relationship into this one. She used to hate doing things, like going for walks with Elaine, because they weren't walks, they were parades. Two lesbians holding hands in public; anybody want to make an issue out of it? Walking in the park or wandering around the market with Denise was a different matter. Sometimes they held hands, sometimes they didn't, unconsciously, naturally.

Of course, she had to adjust to the domesticity of it all. Like no more late-night after-work boozing. Denise wasn't anywhere near extrovert enough to cope with Corrine's scandalous colleagues. Fashion designers were work hard-play hard party animals. So these days she was happy being alone with Denise in the evening, just curled up in front of the television (when Steve wasn't watching 'a Cup match').

She'd also begun to take more of an interest in Denise's work. She used to think computers crushingly boring. Just what the hell does a Systems Engineer do? And was it as exciting as, say, working for a leading fashion house? She was changing her view because she began to see Denise's job as more than something that simply buggered up their plans. Denise had a pager and a mobile phone, she was always on twenty-four hour call. Corrine began to realise that, in effect, Denise never actually stopped working. Denise's job was pedantic, exacting, unpredictable and, more often than not, intense. Away from work she desperately needed to unwind and relax. She needed to do this with someone loving, earnest and undemanding — Denise needed her. And it was nice being needed.

What was the time? Half six. She didn't feel too put out at playing the housewife. And anyway, she'd have to get used to this. Hopefully, in the not too distant future, she'd be a mum. She'd be the mother of Steven's child. She'd have a hold over him. A hold that would destroy forever Denise's crush on him...

She went into the kitchen. Moments later she heard the front door being slammed shut. Those were Denise's angry steps pounding up the stairs. The angry steps stormed into the flat and made directly for the kitchen. A momentary glance told her Denise had been crying with rage. Her handbag, briefcase and little computer were thrown onto the sofa. Normally, Denise handled that damn computer as if it were made from crystal glass. Corrine reached out to her.

"I spoke to Jo today," Denise ranted through gritted teeth. "She… she said… You couldn't just…"

Oh.

"Why… why did you have to?"

Oh shit. "What did Jo say?"

"You… you… you just had to do it, didn't you?" said Denise, now shaking with anger.

Shit. Shit. Shit. "Denise, that all happened before I met you," she said measuredly.

"Before—"

"Or at least before I got this flat, before I'd sorted out my life. It was just when we started seeing each other. I was really messed-up. She was a shoulder to cry on."

Denise dropped her hands by her sides and opened-mouth staggered backwards.

Hands outstretched, Corrine took some steps towards her. "I love you. I do."

"You've been with Jo? I thought you said you wouldn't!" Denise pushed out with her arms, almost knocking Corrine over.

"I didn't tell you because…"

"What do you take me for?"

It took a little while for it to register that Denise's words were a question not a statement. "What exactly did Jo say?"

Denise threw up her hands in resignation and plonked herself on the nearest chair. "This just about caps it. You're all the fucking same!" She gave her a long, hard stare. "You slept with Jo. How could you?"

She tried to return the stare. "Yes, only a couple of times. At the very beginning of our relationship. We weren't even going out properly. Not like we are now."

Leaning forward, Denise buried her face in her hands. Corrine wasn't sure if she was crying, laughing or what. She wasn't sure if she should go over to her. Eventually Denise stood, gathering handbag, briefcase and computer.

"What did Jo say?"

"She said that Steven was going to insist on 'donating' to both us us — unmechanically. Because you suggested it."

Shit.

With a final pained smile Denise turned to leave the kitchen. The flat door opened and closed. Denise waited silently. "You pervert," were the words that hit Steve as he entered.

"How long does it take to pack a rucksack, then clean a room?" she asked sweetly, pressing her point.

"What's this? What's goin—"

"Well, Steve?" she asked calmly. "Cat got your tongue?" she taunted. "This threesome you're planning, good story for a night out with your mates, is that it?"

Looking down at his feet, he shuffled from side to

side like a schoolboy caught scrumping. Eventually he looked her in the eye but didn't speak. Denise's head continued its rhumba.

"Well?"

His gaze went to the ceiling. "It's not like that," he laughed, then said, "I didn't mean to stress you out. I can't say anything else except sorry." His eyes went back to his feet.

"Rather elaborate, wasn't it?"

He shrugged.

"So, you're insisting on both of us?" Denise asked.

"Come on, no, of course not. What do you take me for?"

Denise turned to Corrine then back to him. "Then why did you...?"

"It was just a spur of the moment thing. I figured you'd go ballistic." Grinning embarrassedly, he added an afterthought, "Didn't expect to get branded a perv, though."

"So, you don't want to go through with it?" Corrine asked.

"I saw it as a way out," he said earnestly. "Look, Corrine, you want a baby so much, you make it hard for me to say 'no'. Maybe I just need time..."

"You haven't answered my question."

He stared long and hard at them then said, "I'll do it... that is, if you still want me to."

"Denise, do we?" With that she was asking two

questions.

Turning to her, Denise asked back, "When at the beginning of our relationshp... I mean with... When exactly?"

"First couple of days after we met." It was more like a couple of weeks and probably some overlap, but Denise didn't need to know that.

Denise turned back to Steve. "Yes, we still want to. And don't ever think you can pull a stunt like that again."

Steve grinned again, retreating to the door. "I always have problems dealing with brainy women."

With this backhanded compliment, he disappeared before either of them could reply. No sooner had he departed than Denise continued her questioning.

"Why didn't you tell me about Jo?"

"At first, because I didn't want you thinking there was still anything between us. Remember, it was she who introduced us and you were her friend. I didn't know you well enough, I suppose. Then, well, once one tells a lie, one has to live that lie."

Denise was moodily silent for a while. "Did you tell her not to say anything to me?"

"I didn't have to."

She was silent for slightly longer. "Anyone else I should know about?" she asked, half joking.

"No, no one." Not strictly true, but surprisingly, she felt a great sense of relief now that the main thing was out in the open.

Denise seemed to accept that. "What are we going to do about him?" She thrust her chin at the door.

"Are you still attracted to him?"

"No, of course not. But I guess I'm jealous of the thought of him sleeping with you."

"There is no need to be." She was going to say, if he were a woman, then she'd have something to be jealous about. That wouldn't have been very wise in this situation. So, she left it at that.

"I know, but it's how I feel. Don't you feel the same about, well, our past?"

"I suppose so," she agreed. In truth, she couldn't see anything about the legendary Steve to be jealous about. He wasn't exactly anything to write home about. Instead she reassured Denise that it wasn't about Steve or anybody else, it was about them. They were becoming a family, they were in love with each other, deeply, and nobody — "Nobody!" — could come between them.

Denise suddenly laughed, "You should have heard Jo. She was all for coming round to help us geld him."

eight

Why was she so excited? She hadn't anticipated feeling
like this. Nervous certainly, but excited? Daily she'd
watched Corrine take her temperature. Yesterday, today
or tomorrow were always the most likely days. But they
hadn't discussed the details, like whose room?
Ceremonial meal, a few glasses of wine? Or just
winging it? Should she make herself scarce? This she
put to Corrine, who answered, "Don't be silly, I want
you here." It was said as an instruction.

Today was the day, but Steven had already left by the
time it was confirmed. She went to work and
distractedly pottered about until about four, then came
home, excited, anxious, ready.

Just as well she was there. Corrine was so focused
that she was all set to have a shower then just waltz into
his room and announce that her temperature was right.
Indirectly, Denise floated the idea that maybe she ought
to 'prepare' herself. Taking the hint, Corrine went to sit
at the dresser and apply some make-up. She whinged

about it. Denise would prefer her to wear make-up all the time but Corrine made such an issue out of it she kept her own counsel on this.

Then she had to suggest, ever so tactfully, that sweatshirt and jeans were, perhaps, not the best attire. "Well, what should I wear?" Corrine griped. Denise pulled out a baby doll nightie. Corrine pulled a face, "I think you're making too much of this. That would just encourage him." Denise felt like saying, 'I think that's the general idea', but she didn't. They settled on one of her stretched lace bodices that would just about fit Corrine.

Corrine spied herself in the mirror and complained that she looked like Barbie. She went to the drawer and took out a pair of fingerless leather gloves. Denise had to inform her that, even though she liked it, he might not. She didn't have to say anything about hair; Corrine dashed back into the bathroom and returned with her hair gelled back. All in all, Corrine looked, and smelled, deliciously sexy, so damn sexy that she could feel herself getting aroused. They heard Steven come in, but tonight was one of his football training nights. He had a set routine; he'd have a quick snack then spend all night in his room — presumably resting after all that physical exertion.

They had a kiss and cuddle while they waited for him. It began to develop into something more. Denise felt that now Corrine was in the mood she should go to him. "Remember, he's a man; don't be too assertive to begin with." She made a crack. "At least you can tell him with total honesty that he's the biggest and best you've ever had." She suspected that, under the show of bravado, Corrine was really nervous, terrified even. Just as Corrine was about to leave, she went to put on that boring old dressing gown. Stopping her, Denise gave her a silk wrap. They had a long parting kiss.

As Corrine gently closed the door behind her, Denise reflected that she'd slept with nine men atogether, had had long-term relationships with four, and had lived with two. Complete disasters all of them. She'd always put the failures down to the men, figuring that she was attracted to the wrong sort. She knew that she had a strong sex drive, but it wa easier to blame them for her lack of sexual gratification. With Steve, who had taken her virginity, sex had been something different: wildly exciting, steamily passionate, deliciously delightful, and deeply satisfying. That's why she used to like frolicking with him so much.

It wasn't 'till Edwin had slapped her around; she packed her bags, walked, and went to cry on a friend's shoulder that things began to unravel. It was while she was literally crying on Yvonne's shoulder that she found herself getting aroused. Of course she didn't know how to deal with it. Nothing in her experiences even hinted at this and she had known several gay women. Surely your true sexual orientation can't sneak up on you.

How could she not have known what it was from the outset? Corrine knew right from puberty which way she swung. Why did it take a beating from Edwin, when she was twenty-nine, before she understood why her ship never came in? Why she had never had an orgasm during intercourse. But that didn't matter with Steve. He was always the exception, the only man who could make her reconsider.

Yes, she conceded, she was probably 'slightly' bisexual. To prove it was only 'slight', she dropped her drawers at the slightest provocation. Five times. Five meaningless, dissatisfying one-night stands. Those five convinced her that maybe, just maybe, she wasn't 'slightly' bisexual after all. But now Steve was back in her life, and she wasn't so sure any more.

***

Crashed out on his bed wearing T-shirt and pants, Steve rested aching limbs, his mind floating. There was a slight knock at the door, then Corrine stepped in. He had to sit up. Bolt upright, in fact. His mouth sagged open. This was not the same Corrine. Her hair, her make-up, and no glasses. Under a see-through scarf she had on a red see-through swimsuit-type thing with black trimmings. He sat there gaping. She still wasn't in Marti's league but she could easily give Babs a run for her money. This only went to confirm his suspicion that she'd look seriously criss if she bothered.

Things were just about to start happening in the pants department when she had to go and spoil it.

"I'm ovulating," she said in the same tone a wife does when saying, 'The grass needs cutting'. Then lumbered over to him.

He felt like saying, 'You don't walk like that when you're wearing clothes like those'. She stopped about a foot away and just stood there looking down at him with no particular expression on her face. Considering her proximity, her attire, her large tits and exposed flesh, nothing was happening down below. He sat there undecided, realising that he hadn't really thought this through. He knew what they'd agreed, but now it was for real.

In those brief moments while he deliberated on his next move, she took a deep breath and stared off over his head. Shaking off the wrap, she undid (with surprising ease and speed) the swimsuit then stepped out of it. *No, no, no. You don't do it like that.*

"Can I turn off the light now?" Her eyes were back on his. He knew that expression, he'd seen it often enough — Five minutes to Drop Zone. You're hooked up, line checked, 145 pounds of kit plus two parachutes strapped to you. Left for five minutes with your own thoughts, usually about your own mortality. Five minutes before the bravado and bullshit started. Five minutes before you stepped out of an aircraft.

"I'd prefer if they were turned off."

"It's all right," said Steve, brushing past her, "I'll do it."

What he needed was to buy himself some time. Flicking the switch, he noted that it hardly made a difference. The curtains were drawn but it was pretty bright outside. Turning round he saw that she was now lying on the bed. Just that, naked on the bed, staring at the ceiling. He hesitated for a moment then took off his T-shirt and tossed it on a chair. Trying to get his brain out of neutral and focusing on her tits, he started over. As he came into view she moved her eyes, but not her head, to look up at and through him. He took time to thoroughly scan her body, feet to head; legs, thighs, hips, waist, breasts, shoulders, face. All wickedly nice. But...

She seemed surprised to find him looking down at her, decided that he must be waiting for something. Mechanically she moved her legs apart. His move, he supposed. He pulled off his pants, revealing a respectable erection. Her eyes never left his. This he didn't believe. Women always checked out the equipment. So, there he was, standing, naked. There she was, lying, naked. But...

She flashed him a sort of reassuring smile, and he wouldn't have been surprised if she'd said, 'Don't worry, it's not going to be that bad'. He didn't need reassurance, but it might have eased the tension if the smile lasted. It didn't.

A moment later, he was kneeling between her legs. This was the kind of position he used to spend a lot of time, energy and effort to be in. But she didn't move, she didn't react. She just continued to stare at him. He could smell her perfume. As a rule, he wasn't that hot on perfume — he liked his women raw — but what she was wearing was nice, not sickly sweet at all.

Now, over the years, he'd perfected dozens and dozens of 'lines' to use in just this type of situation. Unfortunately, none of the ones that came to mind was appropriate.

Something had to be said. He couldn't just go along with this 'Here I am, now fuck me', attitude, could he? Having knelt there for a good second or two, with his brain refusing to work, he figured he might as well get on with it. As he lent forward to get on top of her, she tensed. He wouldn't go as far as saying her expression changed to one of absolute horror, but it wasn't far from it either.

He started to lean back, "I…" She grabbed his hand to keep him there. He stopped, uncertain. She moved her legs further apart, as if that should help him make up his mind. It might have, except he could feel her shaking. That made up his mind.

"I'm sorry, but I can't."

"What do you want me to do?" she seemed genuinely puzzled.

"What?"

"If this isn't how you want me you have to let me know."

"I don't believe I'm hearing this... All right, all right, never mind." He'd fucked enough women to just get this over and done with. But wasn't she supposed to be 'wet and wanting'? At least Corrine was wet. He'd expected that to be a problem and at some other time he'd try and figure out why it wasn't. He'd had more difficulty with women who were gagging for it. 'Wanting?' Definitely not. She didn't react as, slowly and as gently as he could, he slid into her. She just lay there, one hand by her side, the other gripping his arm.

Now, I've never fucked a blow-up doll, but it must be a bit like this.

This was positively the worst time for such a thought to surface. It was going to take him forever to come, if at all. Funny; how often had he been with a woman who wanted him to 'keep it up all night' and he couldn't? Now, here he was with Corrine who, if he could come right then, would have been well happy, and he couldn't.

He figured that the only way to get through this was to focus on her tits and not worry about what was going on down below or up top. In an unconscious sort of way, deed followed thought. His hand started kneeding her tits. In what was probably also an involuntary act, she grabbed his hand to stop. Seeing the utter disappointment on his face, she relented.

"Easy. They're tender," she explained.

Bollocks.

"Corrine this is kinda stressful for both of us. So, I've got an idea."

Her expression was a mixture of curiosity and suspicion. "What is it?"

"You want me to come right now, don't you. I don't think…"

"I don't expect you to come right now. That's too soon, isn't it?"

"Yeah, but what I'm trying to say is, I don't think I'm going to for a long time."

"Lucky you…" She had a eureka look about her. "What you're saying is that you need more enthusiasm from me, yes?"

He couldn't believe he was having this conversation in this situation. "Yeah, and…"

"OK then," she said all boisterous and jolly hockey sticks.

With one hand she seized him around the neck and started kissing him. With the other, she took his hand and placed in on her left breast. He went with the flow for a while. Not a bad kiss, great tits, he could get into this…

She pulled away. "You haven't shaved."

"Oh right, sorry." This was laughable.

In the end it was pretty simple really. He started

reliving every moment of sex he'd ever had with a horny woman. Funnily enough, none of them was a babe. As a rule of thumb, women who deliver pure, tear-up sex, weren't necessarily fantastically good looking. Of course, there were exceptions to every rule. Marti came to mind. How could you tell she'd be a good fuck? You just could; the way she stood, the way she moved, everything about her said she'd be a good fuck. Pity about the lesbian bit. Sad about Jo... Denise... What a fucking waste.

So, there he was, riding one woman and having mental sex with several others. Weird as this was, some even weirder things were going down. Like, neither of them made a sound. Eyes shut tight, she kept her lips clamped to his and didn't let out even a peep let alone a moan or a groan. Weirder still, apart from her firm grip on him, it was like she was dead from the neck down. It would have been extremely off-putting, except his mind was elsewhere. Later it would occur to him that her thoughts were probably also elsewhere.

Now, not every woman he'd ever screwed screamed down the house with, 'Oh God Steve! Fuck me! Yes, yes, fuck me!' or words to that effect. Some could be said to be relatively muted. It had taken him most of his early twenties to suss out that he wasn't doing anything wrong, they were just like that. He'd even bonked a woman who said that the way she knew she'd had a really good shag was sweatiness at the back of her knees. But blind drunk or stone cold sober, every woman he'd ever screwed had some reaction to him coming. That was until today.

Nothing. And as he embarked on one of his legendary ten minute orgasms (complete with all the fanfares, drum rolls, rebel yells and moving and grooving), she actually stopped kissing him. As soon as she stopped kissing him, he rolled off her. Without question, that was the worst fuck of his life. But he'd had a lovely time in his head.

He had a pull-down menu of 'nice' things to say immediately after sex as well. However, like his pre-sex banter, none of it was suitable.

Abruptly she sat up. He figured it must have been the worst fuck of her life as well. The only fuck of her life, wasn't it? Worst and best in that case. After all, two women, that doesn't count, does it?

"Gross," she said with feeling, conviction and a shudder.

He sat up, intending to say something along the lines of, 'It can't have been that bad.' But she beat him to it.

"You can't imagine how repugnant I find the thought of your semen inside me. I don't like heterosexual sex. But I can, and will, tolerate it for our child. It's just that... I can't touch it. Why can't I bring myself to touch it?"

Now, in his time he'd come across a number of women who had perfected the art of the one-line killer put-down. This easily topped their best. The only thing he could do was to grin feebly at her.

"Oh. I didn't mean…"

"It's all right, you're a lesbian." Something inside him was having a serious belly laugh.

"Are you mesmerised?" she wanted to know.

"Sorry?"

"You're gawking at my breasts." She gave them a little wobble, not to tease, or tantalise, but to make the point.

"Oh." He hadn't realised he was.

She fixed him with a thoughtful stare. "This one is very sensitive," she pointed to her right breast, the one he had hold of. "I mean, in the erogenous sense. I thought you might… well…" She shrugged apologetically.

He should have read the health warning that sex with a lesbian could seriously damage his ego. He just shrugged back.

"You thought I'd be timid about sex with you, didn't you?"

After sex women were supposed to glow with satisfaction, fulfilment and stuff like that. Here was one glowing with supreme pride. He was too much of a gentleman to say, 'Never mind timid, I've seen more life in a paper plate'. While he sought a diplomatic answer, a word popped into his head — 'courageous'. Yes, what she'd done was brave.

"I hope you get your baby."

Looking at him with an expression he couldn't read, she said, "So do I. But if I don't get pregnant this time, next time it will be easier." Followed by another one of her reassuring smiles.

Next time? Shit. His thoughts hadn't progressed quite as far as a next time, but he nodded.

Ruffling her hair, she said, "Whatever the outcome, thanks. I know it was difficult for you too."

Gratitude was not the usual sentiment in this sort of situation. Difficult? Difficult, wasn't the word he'd use. Again he shrugged.

She pondered for a while. "We could try again later. But to be perfectly honest, I'd rather wait and see."

"Sure." He wasn't going to argue.

"And anyway, it'll take you longer than that to produce fresh sperm."

"No it won't."

"Yes it will," she reaffirmed.

Boy, was she ignorant about men. "A couple of hours, not even that. (If the man knows what he's doing) ten, fifteen minutes."

She gave him an indulging smile. "You might be able to ejaculate again after fifteen minutes but the sperm is immature. And stop staring at my breasts."

He didn't know that. "Sorry. They're pretty distracting," he confessed.

She glanced down at her chest. "Do you really like them? I think they're too big."

She'd reacted like he'd said she had lovely hair. Telling a woman you liked her hair and saying you thought her tits gorgeous, was practically the same thing. That was the root of the problem. All the physical bits were there, but the carnal element was sadly missing.

"Do you normally start again after fifteen minutes?" There was no disguising her curiosity.

What was she after?

"That depends on the woman. Are we comparing notes here?"

"Perhaps."

That was definitely a teasing smile, in no way sexual, but still teasing. He just laughed.

"If I were straight, would you fancy me?"

Women were adept at putting an awful lot of meaning behind simple questions. As usual, he didn't have a clue as to what was really being asked, so he played his ace — his disarming smile. The smile that had gotten him into more knickers than he'd care to remember. "I fancy you right now, exactly as you are."

She didn't exactly blush, but he could see that he'd triggered some emotion. She didn't say anything, but lent across and gave him an affectionate peck on the cheek. Then she got out of the bed, gathered her bits and ambled out. Just that, ambled. Women don't usually walk like that just after sex.

***

She'd done it. She had to deliberately stop herself bursting into the room. Taking a moment to collect herself, she nonchalantly shoved the door open. Looking concerned Denise jumped up as soon as she entered. They ran together and embraced.

"Are you OK?" Denise asked full of concern.

She didn't answer, but instead slipped her hand around Denise's waist and started tugging her playfully towards the bed. Denise submitted to being manhandled but was still worried

"What happened? Why didn't you get dressed?"

"Because I'd only have to get undressed again," she answered suggestively then tipped them both on to the bed and smothered her woman with kisses.

Denise got the message but only just managed to prize herself away, "Have you…?"

"Yes, now come here."

Denise didn't budge. "Shouldn't you have a shower?"

She had a point, but… "I've been looking forward to this for the last fifteen minutes." She pulled her into a tight hug. "It's what kept me going."

Denise seemed hesitant and wouldn't look her in the eye, but with one hand Corrine already had her bra undone and the other was up her skirt pulling off her knickers. They perhaps needed to discuss what had happened. But that would have to wait.

Denise didn't resist but she didn't respond either. In the end she raised her bum so that she could get the knickers off.

"You're a horny bitch," Denise whispered as she pulled the bra off her shoulders, took her hands out and pulled it out through her sleeve.

This was more like it. "Yes, I am *your* HB."

With their legs entwined, they started to kiss deeply. With the door still open.

The knock startled them.

"You left…"

They turned to see Steve; dressing gown on, mouth open, eyes wide, silk wrap in hand. "Sorry, I didn't know… Here's your thing." He dropped the wrap on a chair and sprang back closing the door behind him.

Corrine giggled and turned back to pick up where they'd left off. Denise pushed her away rather forcefully.

"He's an adult. He knows the score," Corrine said.

"Corrine," Denise gave her a gentle shove, "how would you feel if you found someone you'd just made love to, making love to someone else a few minutes later?"

"*Love?* If you're worried about his ego, there's no need to be. He understands."

"Corrine, a man *is* his ego," she said knowingly. "And this isn't just about his ego. I'm not happy about having a buttered bun either."

Corrine laughed. "Spread your legs, babe. Let this buttered bun see your passion hedge."

nine

There had been a subtle but fundamental shift in their precarious little threesome. Though Denise couldn't exactly put her finger on it, Steve's attitude had changed, as if he was trying his damnedest to hide something that was bothering him. And she thought she had a good idea what it was.

It was several days after the event before the three of them were together. "It wasn't as I expected," was Corrine's opening gambit. "What did you expect it to be like?" was his neutral response. With all the subtlety of a motorway pile-up, Corrine launched into her discourse: "Not unpleasant, not very physical, strange, could never achieve an orgasm, different…" etc etc.

Denise watched his reactions closely. He kept a tight grip on his expressions, making only minimal comments. By the end, they all knew Corrine's thoughts but had got nothing from him. She could hazard a guess as to why Corrine was doing this. It was her way of showing Steve that sex with a woman was superior, far superior, to anything a man could offer, and to reassure her that it would not develop into anything more.

From that day on, whenever the three of them were gathered, Corrine would invariably turn the conversation to sex. She felt free to not only discuss, but also to compare, what sex was like with both of them. These 'chats' were much the same as the chats they had about gay and lesbian issues.

To his credit, Steve didn't try to steer the conversation away nor did he sit in silence, but what Denise saw was a man slowly withdrawing inside himself. Whenever Corrine started sharing her new found knowledge of sex with a man, he would casually get up and say, "I'm going out, I'll catch you later."

***

Now the test was white, Corrine wasn't pregnant. She had to get to him before Corrine did. He was a creature of habit, he stuck to his routines. She set her ambush — Thursday night.

She heard the front door close and his irregular footsteps. Why did he play football when he always ended up limping? The steps stopped momentarily for him to throw his bag in his room, then continued down the corridor. The kitchen door opened.

"Hi. I've just made some dinner, would you like some?"

He looked at her, at the set table, then asked, "Where's Corrine?"

Dinner had seemed like the perfect ploy to get them to sit together. She'd cooked for him before, but not since... not recently, at any rate. Of course he'd be suspicious. Why hadn't she thought of that? "You know what it's like. Get in from a difficult day to a note saying she's out for a drink with some friends." A lie to cover her tracks.

"What is it?" Not looking convinced, his nose twitched, like he'd already guessed.

"Not rabbit's food." That was how he described Corrine's cooking.

"Yeah, all right." He limped over to the table, his attitude suggesting that he was still wary of greeks bearing gifts.

She brought over the two plates of steaming stewed peas and rice. Sitting, he looked down at his plate then back up at her. Her mind momentarily flashed to her mother, who had patiently taught her to make it. Back to a time when she was still the apple of her mother's eye...

"You came in from a hard day's graft then just threw this together, did you?"

He knew she knew that he liked stewed peas and rice — a dish that you couldn't just 'throw together'. He wasn't dumb, lots of life's experiences under his belt, he wasn't the same eighteen-year-old that she'd known.

She should remember that.

"We need to talk," she confessed.

Surprise, surprise. "What about?"

Fixing an amused expression on her face she answered, "Corrine isn't pregnant."

He just snorted and looked at his plate.

"Steven..."

"Don't call me that."

"Steve, tell me I'm wrong, but I feel that there's a lot that you aren't saying."

"Like what?"

This was exactly the kind of response he had to Corrine talking about sex — short sentences composed of monosyllabic words. So defensive. "We don't want you to feel excluded. We appreciate that you must find it difficult. Which is why we want to be open about everything."

"Yeah, so?" He took up a fork.

She moved to sit opposite. "You haven't. I don't know how you feel."

"Well, maybe... maybe women just like talking about these things. Well, you lot do at any rate."

She wasn't sure exactly what he meant by, 'you lot'. "Don't men talk about, 'these things'?"

"You mean men talking to each other?" he grinned.

"Yes."

"Well, yes. But it's not the same."

The worst thing she could do right then was to get

annoyed. "Why is it not the same?"

His grin widened. "Well, first you have to take half of what they say and toss it straight out the window. And then only believe five per cent of the rest."

"Why?"

"Because no matter what they say, if it's not an outright lie, then it is most definitely an exaggeration," he started to titter. "I tell you, when men talk about sex, it's not the same way you do." Now he was laughing. "Bwoy, the places I hear men say the clitoris is."

The clitoris? "I don't understand. Are you saying men find it difficult to express their feelings about sex without exaggerating?"

"No," he looked perplexed. "I'm saying I can't deal with the way you just drop things — boof!"

"I still don't understand."

"You don't understand? I'm sitting right there in the room and Corrine is talking to Jo on the phone and says, 'I thought it might be uncomfortable, his penis isn't small. But it wasn't the least bit unpleasant'. I'm sitting there thinking, 'Excuse me? Am I in the same room or what? She can't say that'. And anyway, what does she mean by, 'not small'?"

The next worst thing she could do right then was laugh. "That wasn't derogatory…"

"That was nobody else's business."

"Rubbish. That's all you men ever talk about. That's all I hear at work."

"Yeah, but only if she's a coyote," he ungraciously conceded.

"A coyote?"

"Yeah, you know. The kind of woman who, if you woke up and found her lying on your arm, you'd gnaw it off to get away from her."

"You are all such bastards! How can you say that about someone you'd slept with?"

"The point is we wouldn't say it, if she was standing there in the same room. We'd do it behind her back." Shaking his head grouchily he tucked into his meal.

"At least you know how Corrine feels and…"

"Look, I'm not the only one who hasn't said much, right?" Waving his fork like a wand he continued, "You ain't exactly been chatty about it yourself."

No, she hadn't been but this wasn't about her. "You know what I want, don't you?"

Twisting his head to the side he put down his fork and stared penetratingly into her eyes. "What do you want, Denise?"

"I want to know how you really feel about attempting to father our child." Having just given him a lecture on being honest, the word 'hypocrite' sprang to mind.

"And because you want to know that, you just mention in passing that Corrine isn't pregnant, right?"

"I thought you would want to know." This lie sounded hollow even to her ears.

"All right, what precisely do you want to know?" His expression said he didn't believe a word she'd said.

She'd just have to brazen it out. "When we try to talk to you about it, you don't say very much. Why is that?"

"That's because I don't want to talk about it. And I don't want other people talking about it either."

"Why not?"

"I can't just sit there and talk to you and Corrine about it. It's not, like, we're talking about the weather or something. It just doesn't feel right."

"I don't see why not."

"Denise, do me a favour. Don't treat me like a fucking idiot. You don't want to talk about it either. You didn't want to know the 'details', did you? Did you really want me to know what it feels like to have you licking out her snatch? So, stop pissing about. One last time, what do *you* want?"

There was something about the way he'd said that which demanded total candour.

"I... I feel there is something going on that you aren't saying."

He made a pretty good job of suppressing a smile. "You worried I might convert Corrie?"

Stupid man. "No, Steve. But I think you're suppressing... something."

Raising an eyebrow, he grinned. "I'm not falling for her, if that's what you're getting at."

She got the impression that he knew exactly what she

was after but was going to let her work to get it. She'd
see about that.

"How do you feel about walking in on us when we
were getting off with each other?"

"You should do more of the cooking, this isn't bad."

No way was she going to let him blatantly ignore her
question. "Is it only my cooking you prefer?"

Resting his chin on his fist, he stared across at her,
smouldering and thoughtful. Eventually he said, "What
I feel for you hasn't changed, nor will it. But, and I mean
this in the nice sense, I'm not after you — anymore. I
know the score. I don't know how I got into this and I
don't know if I can carry on."

That was more or less what she thought. "Why can't
you carry on?"

Still smouldering he looked even more thoughtful.
"Let's just say that the old ego has taken a serious
battering in more ways than one. But you already know
that, otherwise you wouldn't be asking about how I feel,
right? What do *you* want from me, Denise?"

"What I want is for you to spell it out."

Taking a long slow breath, he launched into his
explanation. "Well, I don't like being the friendly
neighbourhood sperm donor. I don't like Corrine going
on about it like I'd helped her fix her car. I don't like
people knowing about it. And I don't like you, my ex-
girlfriend, playing the anxious expectant father, fussing
over me."

"What about finding us together?"

"What about it?"

"Didn't that… bother you?"

"No, why should it?"

"Come on, be honest."

"I was a bit surprised, then thought about it. Why should I be surprised? You're lesbians for fuck's sake. That's what lesbians do."

"Didn't you mind?"

"Mind? She's your girlfriend, why should I mind?"

She'd expected him to mind. He should mind. He would mind if Corrine had been a man. Why did that infuriate her so much? Was it possible that she'd been barking up the wrong tree? "So why don't you think you can carry on?"

"I've just told you."

"Tell me again," she wanted to be absolutely sure she understood.

"I feel like a tool, right? Not a nice feeling…"

She opened her mouth to protest, but he cut her off.

"I know what you're going to say — that men are mercenary in their dealings with women, so no big deal. That we treat women like walking orifices, right? So what? You know the score; doesn't matter what bollocks a man talks, you know he's after your body. Simple. This is different. It's doing my head in. How would you like it if I said to you, 'Excuse me, madam, though I am aware of your lovely tits, shapely arse, pretty face and gorgeous legs, let me assure you, my interest in you, rests purely in your eggs'."

What? "So, it *is* me you want?"

"Jeeeez!" He buried his face in his hands. "I was just making a point. I *don't* want you."

"Oh."

"Yeah. You've asked me some questions. I've answered them. Now can we drop this?"

She decided not to push it. "OK."

***

"Denise, are you suggesting that I have sex with him even when I'm not ovulating?"

"Certainly not." A look of deep offence.

"Would it help if I spoke to him?"

"I don't know."

Corrine could really do without this. Steve had them dangling on a string, forever changing his mind and then changing it back again. He was playing games. What did he want from them? They were already accommodating his every whim as it was. It was imperative that she kept him interested. Particularly with the news that her first sexual encounter with him had been a dry run. If she didn't know better she would think that he was exploiting the fact that they would have to be at his beck and call and pander to his desires until she was well and truly pregnant.

"I'll go speak to him." She didn't wait for an answer.

After knocking on his door, she gently pushed it ajar.

With Walkman headphones on, lying on his belly, Steve was reading a book. Standing motionless for a few moments, she watched him. Reading? She'd never seen him pick up a magazine or newspaper the whole time he'd been there. Whatever it was, he was totally immersed in it, his head nodding in time to music.

"Steve, a word." She nudged him.

In one smooth motion he looked round, sat up, slipped the book under his pillow and pulled off the headphones. "Tell me you're not going to do my head in," he said.

"I'm not going to do your head in." Smiling she advanced into the room and sat next to him. "What were you reading?"

"A book." He managed to look guilty and suspicious at the same time.

Their shoulders were touching, this was the closest they had been since... then. "A book about...?"

"Pregnancy," he answered matter-of-factly. Pulling it out, he handed it to her.

Pregnancy Book by the Health Education Council. She'd read it.

"Who'd believe that joining a library would be so much fucking hassle," he ventured.

"Why are you reading it?"

"Interesting subject, more to it than I thought. Now,

what aren't you going to do my head in about?"

"Intent."

It took him a moment to comprehend. "Yes, I can definitely feel brain damage coming on. This must be 'Give Steve a Hard Time Week'."

"I'm not giving you a hard time. You know I'm not pregnant. So, before... the next time, I want to know what, if anything, you'd like to be different."

"Hey?"

"What are you into?"

"What?"

"We could... experiment. I'm not inhibited."

"Jesus! Can you... can you... not be so up-front? 'Nurses uniform, a little S&M, how about handcuffs?' Women just don't do things like that. Not even when I'm dreaming. Normally you don't even get a sniff of what they really want until they know you good. And then only if they really trust you."

Was that so? If it was, then there seems to be an awful lot of beating around the bush, so to speak, in heterosexual relationships. Interesting. "I got the impression you wanted things spiced-up."

"Where did you get that from?" Suddenly calm and pensive, he turned to face her. "OK. Say blow jobs are my thing. I know that kinda defeats the object of the exercise, but say as a warmer-upper. How about that?"

She wasn't sure just how hypothetically to take the question. "A blow job?" Having a man's penis in her mouth was beyond her capacity to imagine. There was a world of difference between asking a woman to take his prick in her mouth and using it to facilitate impregnation. _He's not getting a blow job from me._ Was he circumcised? _I hear it makes all the difference._ Why should that make a difference? _Hygiene and, apparently, increased sensitivity._ Pulling a face, she gulped. He had the power to make her do it. "It's all about male domination, isn't it?" Obviously she wouldn't want him to come in her mouth. "OK, I'll do it."

"Sweet." Rubbing his hands together he continued enthusiastically. "But only as a warmer-upper you understand. Then doggy style?"

Staring into his eyes, she sought some sign, even the faintest nuance that he was jesting. There was none. "Providing it does not harm or degrade me... anything." She just managed to keep her voice steady.

In a flash he was on his feet staring down at her. "I'm going to the pub." Then he was bounding towards the door.

"Steve."

"I can't deal with this. I'm going to the pub," he answered without halting or turning.

"Steve."

At the door he stopped and turned slowly to face her, an unreadable expression on his face. "I knew you would do my head in." A measured delivery.

"Please come and sit back down."

Hesitantly he shuffled back to the bed and sat as far as he could from her. "I don't want things spiced-up. What I want... would like, I can't have. So there is no point in thinking or talking about it, OK?"

"What would you like?"

"Didn't you hear what I just said?"

"Yes, but I'd like to know."

"Corrine, look, the only way I can carry this off is to forget that you're a lesbian. But everything you and Denise do reminds me that you are. You understand? With normal women you just don't sit around and talk about things like this. You don't discuss, you don't explain, you don't analyse. What you do is do, and have a hell of a lot of fun in the process."

She will allow him this one 'normal'. "So, you want to play sex games?"

"No." He looked about to tear his hair out. "I'll do it again. Okay? I will do it, just leave me alone. God. Tell these women to leave me alone. You really want to do something for me, Corrine? Can you turn yourself into a heterosexual?"

"No."

"Well then."

Why all the fuss? "I'm still a woman."

Taking a deep breath, he became slightly more serious. "Before you say another word, let me explain one more time. I know you are a woman, a criss woman. But I can't have a good time if you don't have a good time. No matter what I do, you ain't gonna have a good time — you are a lesbian. Understand?"

"Of course I understand, I don't expect to enjoy it."

"Thank you very much. So let's just get on with it. OK? Without passion, without warmth, without mutual appreciation, without the fun. No point trying to bonk each other's brains out. Noooo, I don't think so."

"I think I understand now," she said. "If I were making love to a woman who was frigid, that would be a problem."

"Would it?"

"For sure. OK. I'll see what we can do about 'intent'." She stood and headed for the door.

***

"We have an idea," Corrine said from behind him that next Sunday morning.

All he wanted was to eat his cornflakes in peace. His knee was killing him and he had a match in exactly two hours. The pain in his knee would go once he'd warmed up. Unfortunately there didn't seem to be a way to get rid of these two pains in the arse. Why didn't they just drop it? He was almost afraid to turn round, but did. They were both standing there, bright and breezy. However, the look on Denise's face said that this was Corrine's show. At least he'd had nearly a whole week without any nonsense.

"Yeah? Why don't you tell me all about it?" He settled back for more lesbian-induced grief.

Corrine darted over and pulled out the chair next to him. Denise proceeded more leisurely, she sat opposite; definitely not her show.

"Why don't we make it a game?" Corrine started excitedly.

"A game?"

"Yes," Corrine looked to Denise for support. "We're all adults here. Everybody plays games."

"What type of game?" The cornflakes suddenly lost their flavour.

"We could call it, 'Steve's babe'."

"Right, *and*…?"

"You paint for us the picture of your ideal woman and I'll try and be her."

"How is that going to solve the underlying problem? That's a bit like acting out fantasies, isn't it?"

"Exactly, that's what sex games are for," said Corrine.

"Let me see if I got this straight in my head. I tell you who my ideal woman is and you'll pretend to be her, is that right?"

"Yes. I think I'd enjoy being her."

Here he was, put off his breakfast, and trying his damnedest not to laugh.

This must be a dream. He wondered if they'd find it strange if he pinched himself. "Ahhh, Corrine might find it a little difficult. My ideal woman's black."

"So, star, yuh nuh t'ink me can step forward as a sistren?"

Corrine's switch from sloaney to bashment gal was so startling he cracked up. She was like a female Ali G. Alison G, perhaps. After he'd done rolling around, he said, "You been hanging with the wrong people. Anyway, she isn't a rasta woman."

"Who is she?" Denise seemed well curious.

"Well," Steve mused, "she's number one, the top woman, the goddess, the carnival queen. If you don't know who she is, find out. Now, I've got to go. See you later."

Fast as he could, he got out of the kitchen before he wet himself laughing. One day he would have to share this with Andy.

ten

Why Merlene Ottey? t was surely an insight into his psyche. If she were given the chance of choosing any woman, Merlene Ottey wouldn't be her top choice. She wouldn't even be in her top ten. In her top one hundred possibly, but low down, like in the high nineties. Corrine had set her the task of getting Merlene's photo, which was now blu-tacked to their bedroom wall. Why was she bothered that he hadn't chosen someone who looked more like, well, her?

Corrine set about becoming Merlene Ottey. She proved to be resourceful. The very next day she appeared with a video of Merlene being interviewed. Later she would start going to the gym and visiting a solarium to darken further her already dark skin.

'Tonight Matthew, I'm going to be Merlene Ottey with stars in my eyes!'

This was a game far too good to squander on Steve. Denise and Corrine had now been together just long enough for sex to start becoming routine. Corrine's Merlene changed all that, routine went out the window.

Over the next few days Denise found, even at work, she'd be thinking about going home to make love to 'Merlene'.

As for Steve, he seemed oblivious to the outbreak of Lycra. Denise knew he hadn't noticed because she was watching him like a hawk. But notice he most certainly would. Corrine was ovulating.

"What do you think?" said Corrine, turning to reveal a tiny belly button on a flat*ish* stomach. She had on the half vest with shorts cut high on the hips, accentuating her waist.

"Are you wearing any knickers?"

Suggestively hooking a finger under her crotch, Corrine indicated that she wasn't. "So, what do you think?"

Her thought at that precise moment was that a couple of weeks ago she could never have imagined Corrine wearing bright coloured nail polish. Corrine was looking good, and she didn't want her to get off with Steve again. But she said, "Yes. That's it."

"Are you sure?"

"Absolutely."

"Get out, go," she shooed her away from the mirror. "And I want you back dressed exactly as you are."

***

She didn't knock, just pushed the door open. "Steve,

fancy a few laps round the track."

He glanced up, then looked again, his mouth sagging open. Taking that as a positive sign she started over, a perfect imitation of Merlene's slow side to side sexy swagger, "Yes, bwoy, it is that time again."

Blinking so rapidly that she wondered whether he had something in his eyes, he just stared back at her.

"Ah no joke me ah run."

Giving him a smile Merlene would have been proud of, she kept the swagger going. Could she get those dulcet tones just right? "Let's get it on."

Mouth even wider, he slowly rose from the bed scanning her from toe to head and back again. When she reached him, she smiled up as she slipped her hands under his T-shirt, exploring the muscles around his shoulders and back — no need to pretend when everything was pretence. She guessed correctly that if a man desired one of the fittest and fastest women in the world, it was because of her physical prowess. Pressing her stomach against his, she bumped him back to the bed. As he swayed, she grabbed the T-shirt and pulled it off over his head.

Then she forced him to lie back, jumping on top and thrusting her nipples against his. That's what she'd do with Denise and saw no reason why it couldn't apply here. Until that moment she hadn't realised that the expression, 'Flex up yuhself', had sexual connotations — so she flexed. Squeezing him ever so tightly, she slowly ground... Shit. He hadn't shaved.

She kissed him anyway. Merlene wouldn't be satisfied with mere pecking, would she? She stuck her tongue as far into his mouth as she could. Did all men kiss like this, or just him? Or was it that women had much more awareness of the sensuality of the mouth? Concentrate. He wasn't responding as he should, probably still in shock. She moved up to sit across his chest, taking his hands she placed them inside her vest. With his warm hands on her breasts she put her hands behind her neck and waited. Slowly he started teasing her nipples. He was quite gentle really, not at all what she'd expected. Still she waited, nothing. If those had been Denise's hands... *Concentrate.*

She smiled down at him. He just looked up like he still didn't believe this was happening. Suddenly loud soulful music started blasting out from the next room. It sounded like Ronnie Laws — her lover telling her that she was here with her in spirit. Time to get serious. Getting off she sat him up, pressed him against the bed-head and slid onto his lap. Merlene would be physical, very physical. This time he responded to her kiss, he could kiss, not as well as... Concentrate.

Sliding her hand inside the top of his track suit trousers, making sure she had his pants as well, she stood and in one swift motion pulled them off. Then she made a point of tossing them across the room. Stepping up to straddle his outstretched legs, she grabbed her top

and wiggled it off her shoulders and arms — not up,
over her head, but down, over her tits. With it hanging
round her waist, she paused there in all her glory. His
eyes went wild. *Good.* As she moved to get back on him,
his eyes flashed down, hers followed — he didn't have
an erection.

What the hell was she supposed to do? *Blow job!*
What was that he'd said about blow jobs? Frozen to the
spot, she stared down at his flaccid penis. If she couldn't
make herself touch it, how could she take it in her
mouth? She tried, she really did, but she couldn't get
her hands to move. She couldn't bring herself... Their
eyes met, exchanging looks. *What was wrong with him?*

This was the worst moment of his life. But it can't be
him. That had never happened before. There was
nothing wrong with him.

***

Total equipment failure was something that only
happened to other guys, not to him. Brewer's droop?
That was all bollocks — he never got that drunk. So how
did he explain this — a complete shutdown in the man-
machine department? *Merlene or no Merlene, underneath
it all she's still a fucking dyke, that's what.* For some strange
reason this explanation didn't ring true. It's difficult to
lie to yourself. It was like he was running away from
something. What?

It was the day after, and he was trying to focus on work, on fixing cars. There was plenty to do that morning. Tools, oil, men and cussing kept his mind off negative thoughts, doubts.

"It's nearly three and you haven't had anything to eat."

He saw Naheed's legs, knees together, squatting beside the wheel arch. Three? Already? Eat? He was too fucked off to eat. So fucked off that he was ripe for going round to let that bitch Tracy know what was what. He grunted something at Naheed.

"I've just taken the banking. I got you a steak and kidney pie, it was all they had left."

Sliding from under the car, he looked up into a smiling friendly face. He suddenly felt guilty at his brusqueness. "Thanks. How much do I owe you?"

"My treat, I'll put it in the microwave," she said as she stood and strolled away. From his prone position he had a nice view of her incredibly long legs, right up her mini skirt. A view that didn't diminish as she walked between cars, tools and mechanics until she reached the other side of the workshop. He got up, washed his hands then went into what passed for a kitchen. She was still in there, bent over, fiddling with the microwave. Inside his head something went 'click'.

"Fancy going for a drink some time?" When you ask a woman a question like that you've got to sound like you don't care if she says 'no'.

Coyly, she asked, "When, tonight?"

"If you like."

Her face darkened with suspicion. "Just a drink?"

"Yeah, just a drink." He gave her a 'what else could it possibly be?' look.

Her face went back to its normal affable expression. "Straight after work?"

"Makes sense."

"OK, but I won't be finished till around half six."

That was a message that even he understood. The lady was concerned about her already tattered reputation. None of the other guys would be around at half past six. "I'll be here," he said in his best Arnold Schwarzenegger voice.

Flashing him a smile, she departed. His eyes followed her disappearing arse. So, he wasn't going round to see Tracy after all. Grabbing the hot pie he went back to work. Nothing like changing the gearbox on a Citroën to get rid of pent-up aggression. He was looking forward to hammering the shit out of it

Six thirty was announced by the arrival of Naheed's stilettoed feet. *Doesn't time fly when you're having fun?* Pulling himself out from underneath the car he said, "I hope this guy appreciates what a grand job I've done for him." To kill time, he'd also sorted out the brakes.

"It belongs to a woman, Ms Archer."

Not only had she changed her shoes, there were signs of fresh make-up. "Oh right. I'll just go wash up."

She followed, then stood and watched as he stripped to the waist to wash himself. All the while talking pleasantly to him.

She suggested he left his bike; they could come back for it later. He agreed. She was pretty insistent about not going to the nearest pub. He didn't fight it — somebody they both knew might be in there. Instead, she drove him to a quiet old timers' pub up in Camberwell. On the way, he learned that she lived in Herne Hill.

As they settled back over their first drinks it gradually dawned on him that she was even more gregarious out of work. That's just how she was. Now, here was a woman who liked everything about being a woman. He loved women like that.

They chatted away nice and relaxed, slowly drinking their drinks. As usual, vital information was being exchanged. She asked without asking, why he'd waited until now to make his move. His answer to her unasked question was, because he had a girlfriend at the time — he was a one woman man. She said without saying she'd been waiting for that move, and now that he had made it, it should remain secret. And so it went on. Her feeding him the things he needed to know like what she liked doing — clubbing or romantic evenings in. This sounded like a contradiction but he could see why she would like those two extremes. What else did he need to know? She shared a flat with another girl who was a nurse. This flatmate didn't seem to concern her, so he didn't dwell on it. He supposed that two women — two heterosexual women — sharing a flat must have a system going. Between the second and third drink she went outside to make a call on her mobile phone. To whom? Her flatmate, saying, "Get your drawers off the clothes horse, I'm bringing a guy back?"

They were leaving the pub by nine. He was a gentleman, didn't mind that she took the lead. She was like, "We'd better make a move then," out to her car and off they drove. This always fascinated him — getting into the most intimate of situations without a single direct thing being said about it.

When they arrived outside her place, she took his hand in a girlfriend sort of way. Once inside the flat she marched him straight into her room. No cup of tea, or smooch on the couch. It was in through the front door, straight across the sitting room, right into her bedroom — woman on a mission. Then she dived into a drawer, pulled out something pink and said, "I'll be back."

Here was another thing that intrigued him. Things are running along, as sure and true as the Bullet Train, then wham, they disappear into the loo. Why did they always do that? To do what? Why did they always take so long? He looked round the room, not that he was particularly interested. A girlie room. She certainly hadn't anticipated having a guest; the room wasn't a tip but could have been tidier. His eyes settled on a small gold framed poster with foreign writing. The writing could have been Arabic or Indian. He didn't know the difference.

"Do you like silk?"

The way she asked the question hinted that when he turned, he was going to like what he saw. Slowly he turned. She stood by the door in a plain pink nightie that stopped just below her knees. Here was a woman who knew how to do it. No tarty frilly bits to distract the eyes — simple and effective. Her tits stuck out so far that the nightie hung off them like a pink waterfall. Underneath was the silhouette of a perfect hourglass figure, and those long, long legs.

"I think I'm going to."

She gave him a beaming smile then her hand shot out to slap the lights off. It was dark but not so dark that he couldn't see her. She reached him in three strides but didn't hug him as he'd expected. Instead she reached down and yanked the duvet back. Having sorted the bed, she turned her attention to him, stripping him in seconds. She slipped into the bed and he followed. She smelled of coco butter. This was heaven.

"I love the feel of silk against my skin. Cuddle me," she crooned.

Now, one of the things he quickly learned after joining the army was that the image of paratroopers bravely jumping out of aeroplanes was horse shit. He'd been 'assisted' out of a plane on more than one occasion. You don't think about it, you just shuffled up behind the man in front, then out you went. If you're first out, tough. But no one would jump out of a plane if they really, really, really thought about it.

Slipping her legs ever so slowly between his, she kissed his nipples. Then just as slowly she started rubbing herself all over him — nobody was in a hurry to get anywhere. The silk nightie added a new and interesting dimension, better than skin to skin. Kissing her neck, he ran his hands from her shoulder to her calf. By morning he would know her body better than he knew his own. And no doubt, here was a woman who knew how to seriously love-up a man.

But he had a thought. It only lasted a fraction of a second, but still a thought. He knew what he had to do, not panic or worry or get embarrassed. Easy to say but hard to do. Especially when everything was so just right; coco butter, a silken kitten purring in his arms; it doesn't get any better than that. Yet nothing was happening downstairs. Even a gay man should be able to get it up in this situation. He knew what he had to do; don't think about it and it'll happen.

"It doesn't matter," she said softly, as she gently rubbed the useless piece of flesh against his belly.

It does matter. The fact that she didn't seem to mind just made it worse. The ceiling opened and a whole heap of pressure dropped right on him.

It's simple. Don't think about it. How could he not think about it? It was sort of impossible to think about anything other than Naheed in his arms. Attached to these thoughts was that other one… How the fuck was he going to separate them? He should be enjoying every single moment of this. But…

Naheed held his head and unhurriedly guided it where she wanted it. Like she was saying, "Relax. You've still got fingers and tongue, you know."

Well, so he had. He started above the belly button and took his time working down. By the time he got there she was making soft, deep sounds, sounds that let him know he'd hit the spot.

But the thought lingered: here was a spontaneous encounter with a woman who made all the right moves and he was still non-operational.

eleven

How long had they known each other? How long had they been together? Yet only now was she beginning to realise that she'd never seen Corrine really upset. And seeing her in that state made Denise realise that she was completely ill-prepared to play the supportive role. Perhaps not ill-prepared, just out of practice.

From the moment Corrine burst into the room and threw herself into her arms, she should have known this was role reversal. She should have done what Corrine did when she was distressed. But she didn't. Steve must have done or said something to hurt her lover. All she wanted to know was what. Then she'd go give him a piece of her mind. She'd do more than that; big as he was, ex-boyfriend or not, she had no qualms about bottling him.

Yes, Corrine had been almost incoherent, but all she needed to know was what he'd done. So intent was she on venting her fury that she wasn't listening. Instead of being empathetic she was an inquisitor; 'Did he...?' 'Has he...?' 'He didn't... did he?' Buried in her arms,

Corrine sobbed 'No' to each of her questions. Then they heard him leave, slamming the front door behind him. That was the signal for Corrine to decamp to the kitchen. She followed. After a couple of glasses of wine and between sobs, Corrine told her what had happened. Having taken it in, she was simply confused. For the life of her, she couldn't see why Corrine was so upset.

She watched as Corrine drank a whole bottle of wine. Corrine didn't get any clearer, and she didn't get any nearer understanding. After all, if Steve was impotent that was his problem. Why on earth should she be so upset? She couldn't get to the bottom of Corrine's concern.

***

It never rains, it fucking pours. Like he didn't have enough on his plate already. It had been an unbelievable couple of days. Starting with the lack of performance with Corrine. Then what should have been a straightforward mission — shag Naheed. Mission accomplished? Not quite. Lots of making love, till about two thirty, perhaps three in the morning. But no shagging. God had a funny way of paying you back for wickedness.

The alarm went off at six. He awoke, ready for action. She awoke wanting more. Nice. Then it occurred to him that he'd not only satisfied Naheed, but he'd put her to sleep luxuriating in the experience. Except, without using his cock. Wasn't that what lesbians did? Naheed then did something kinda interesting. Snuggling up to him, she said, "She must have really hurt you, whoever she is, but I'm going to change all that."

What did this mean? It meant she was declaring herself his girlfriend — together they would work it out. This was his kind of woman. But there was Tracy, Corrine and Denise to sort out first.

"All right," he managed.

Nestling her head on his breast she hugged him then said, "Steve, have you ever listened to the lyrics of that song *Just Be Good to Me?*"

"Sure."

"Well, that song could have been written for me. I don't need someone with lots of money or anything like that. All I want is someone to be good to me. Steve, will you be good to me?" she asked, staring into his eyes.

"Yes."

Looking like she believed his answer she gave him a 'thank you' kiss. Wonderful.

So on top of everything else, he now had a girlfriend. A girlfriend who required delicate and considered handling. A girlfriend who he shouldn't, and mustn't, mess about. He could almost hear God wetting Himself. Considering she'd spent all night and morning with a guy who couldn't get it up, Naheed was pretty nice to that guy over breakfast. Better than that, she was radiant and made a big fuss over him.

At work this girlfriend business really kicked in. Despite himself, he found his ire rising when he caught the lads' eyes following her arse. The more he tried to ignore it, the worst it got. By the end of the day, layers and layers of tension had been heaped upon the layers and layers of stress.

Simple solution: football practice. Time to let off steam. Yes, it was only practice. Yes, they were on the same team. But the fact of the matter is, Steve was a central defender. Central defenders and centre forwards don't agree. So, the first time the centre forward went past him, he decided that it would be the last. He wasn't going to hurt the guy, he just wanted to let him know (in a firm sort of way) that dribbling past him wasn't on. Not only did this centre forward not get the message, the next time he went to tackle him, he put the ball through his legs — nutmeg.

He bided his time; when the centre forward and ball again came his way, something inside his brain detonated. One minute he was sticking out a foot to take the centre forward's legs from under him. The next, he was writhing round with said centre forward bending over him saying, "Sorry Steve... 'Kin hell. Call an ambulance somebody."

They didn't call an ambulance, they just picked him up and bundled him into a car. He didn't know whose car and he didn't care, he was in agony. It was all a blur from there — casualty, examinations, doctor, student doctors. While they looked his knee over, someone said, "Note the displacement of the knee cap. Almost to the back of the knee? This type of injury we would normally only see in skiing accidents."

Give the doctors their due, they did explain what his injury was and what they were going to do about it. But he wasn't really listening. Then the nurses started looking at him like he shouldn't be bawling the place down. They could look, he didn't care, it wasn't their leg that was killing them.

Now, whatever it was they gave him to wake him up after the operation, really woke him up. He tried to get out of bed, some nurse came and forcefully put a stop to that. Andy was there, so he got him to phone everybody that needed phoning, except Naheed. He'd do that himself.

Andy came back and told him that his mum and dad would come first thing tomorrow. His mother had said she'd make him some gungoo pea soup. He told Andy to split. No point in hanging about, just bring him some clothes and money tomorrow, leave him to think about his next moves... or non-moves.

***

Why the fuck did they wake you up so early? He wasn't going anywhere, he couldn't do anything. So, why didn't they just leave him to sleep? Having woken him, they forced him to eat some horrible food. Then they left him awake, bored and in pain. It was like the army. There was also the small matter of pain killers. What fucking pain killers? They weren't working and she wouldn't give him any more.

Alverna was her name, Bajan, huge tits, about his age. Now, if he wasn't in so much pain, and she wasn't so domineering, and the last couple of days hadn't happened, and he didn't have to behave because of Naheed, she'd be worth getting to know. As it was, the dark recesses of his mind noted that she was cute and left it at that.

About 10.00 a.m. they brought round a pay phone on a trolley. That gave him something to do, like explain to his boss the situation. Well, sort of; he explained to Naheed and then she explained to his boss — much better that way. It was nice having a real babe concerned about your well-being.

With so much time on his hands and nothing to do, his mind rambled: women, football, cars and back to women: from Tracy to Naheed via Katrina, Corrine and Denise. He knew deep down there had to be something else. But whatever it was, he he had yet to imagine it.

The boredom was broken by visits. His mother and father turned up, mum reading his chart with her former nurse's eye deciding that her homemade gungoo pea soup was the key to his recovery. Then Andy must have passed through when he was asleep because he now had some clothes and a huge hardback book about gardening. When he opened the book, a hardcore, totally illegal, porno mag fell out. Here was something he could think about. This type of stunt had been Andy's trademark in the army. Steve could never get his brain round it. Like there you were on exercise, or maybe seeing a little action that doesn't quite make it into the newspapers — you aren't going to get near a woman for weeks, or perhaps, even months. Out of nowhere somebody produces this stuff. Why? Why remind yourself of something you cannot have? Why build up tension when there is no possible release? Why make things worse than they already were? It's not as if it's easy to beat the meat in the gun trench or when you're on a fighting patrol. Carrying porno mags always struck him as just extra weight leading to self-inflicted wounds.

He had another strategy, a superior strategy. Carry a memory, a memory down to the last detail. It didn't matter where he was, or what he was doing, there was always another world he could retreat into. Obviously, this didn't apply to hit and runs. Then you had enough trouble remembering her name. But a woman he'd spent time with, taken time over — he could live off that for weeks.

He'd put it to the test, he knew his strategy was superior. There was that time when they dropped into

Norway. Everybody was so pissed off about Arctic training. A spot of pleasant skiing by all means... The Booty (the Royal Marine) was the type supposed to fuck about in the Arctic, not the Para. Three weeks. Three whole fucking weeks of Arctic warfare; ice trenches, battalion advance to contact, the works. Did he get cold? No, he did not. Did he come down with exposure? Not at all. Why? Because every time he felt the slightest bit cold or uncomfortable, he left the Arctic Circle. He went back to a hot place, a hot memory, in other words to a woman who was hot.

The next afternoon a physio came to see him. For a fleeting moment he thought she was going to make him walk. But no, that would be tomorrow. This was just to introduce herself and outline what the physio treatment was about. Great. Less than 24 hours after his operation they were going to turf him out of bed and get him going up and down stairs — definitely like the army.

Just after seven the monotonous day took a turn for the better. There across the ward smiling at him was Naheed. Her simple smile instantly lifted his spirit. He smiled back. Grinned, more like. She was seriously dressed to impress, hopefully for his benefit.

She'd brought him a little teddy bear and some grapes. A nice touch, without irony. Pulling up a chair, she sat herself down, leant back, crossed her legs, and without saying anything, slipped her hand under the covers, up his gown and got hold of his cock. So, there he was thinking he was in for an unexpected, but much appreciated, hand job, when she suddenly got up, pulled the screen around his bed, placed her hair behind her ears, pulled back the sheet and lowered her head.

It had to be said: there were some women who were incapable of giving a decent blow job even if they had an instruction manual. On the other hand, there were an exceptional few, as he was now beginning to appreciate, who should hand over something to bite on before they got down to it. Their blow jobs were so damned exquisite there was always the danger of a man biting off his own tongue.

Half out of her chair, she had one hand round his cock working the foreskin, and the other round his balls. His head was moving in perfect sync with hers. Please God, don't let anyone come in. To his surprise he was pretty much moaning. Not only that, with his arms he'd raised his backside off the bed, thus placing a certain strain on his injured knee.

"Woooooph!" Now that's what you call a blow job.

Kissing after a blow job was out of the question. Damn stupid. After all, whose cock had her lips been round?

Smiling he leaned forward to meet her half way but she gently pushed him back onto the pillow. What was he missing? She melted in his arms. When they finally separated, she beamed down at him with tears in her eyes. Still with one hand on his cock, still playing with his foreskin, she stepped out of her shoes and started pulling down her knickers with the other hand. She dropped the knickers into her handbag and took out a condom. Because he was so busy looking at the curtain expecting someone to burst through, he missed exactly how she did it, but she opened the packet and slipped it on with only one hand. What a show stopper. You could dazzle a man to death with that move. That was badder than a cowboy riding his horse, pouring tobacco and rolling a cigarette with one hand. Slick! He'd have to get her to show him.

She hoisted herself onto the bed. Taking care to avoid his leg, she straddled him and guided him into her, smiling.

Considering the situation, she didn't appear to be in any hurry. She tried to kiss him but he was starting to get severe neck ache from looking round so fast and so often. Time was of the essence. Hands up her blouse, he didn't bother undoing her bra, he just lifted her tits out. She had his lips pressed tight against an erect nipple and took her time grinding up to speed. Was it that she was really quite strong, or was it that women found extra strength when they got on top? This cannot be happening, he thought. And he just knew that this woman was gonna let rip. Bad knee or no bad knee, he didn't have much choice about responding either, already giddy from the heat and the sweet smells radiating from her. Then of course, she had to start moaning.

This is a hospital ward. Shut up, woman. At least the bed wasn't creaking. God, was this woman strong.

He felt, rather than heard, the deep, deep, back of the throat moans as she came. *Someone must have heard.*

She dismounted and started to sort out her hair and clothing, then rearranged the covers. He grinned at her like a kid who had just got his bestest present ever.

With a tissue, she pulled off the condom and wrapped it.

"Told you I'd make you forget about her," she said, self-satisfied.

She gave him a peck on the cheek. "I'll come tomorrow."

"Please, baby please," he grinned again. "Naheed…"

"Yes?"

"There's a lot I want to tell you…"

"But…?"

"You know what I want to say, don't you?"

She gave him another quick peck. "Of course, honey."

Top woman. She pulled back the screen. To his relief, nobody seemed to be paying them much attention, except for the guy in the bed opposite who was looking over giving him the 'you lucky bastard' look. As he watched Naheed saunter sexily out of the ward, his heart jumped. The cause wasn't love but the unmistakable clip, clip, clip of Denise's high heel shoes coming down the corridor. Just like Andy was a walking encyclopaedia of football, Steve remembered every detail about a woman, down to the way they walked. And if Denise had walked in two minutes earlier... *Jeeeeez!* It didn't bear thinking about. Folding his arms, he put his bored face on and started staring at the opposite wall.

***

"Not wishing to rush you or anything, but when will you be better?"

Turning to Carrine he responded with, "Do you mean when will I be able to walk or when will I be able to... sort out Merlene?" He was desperately trying not to laugh.

She shared the joke too. "Wonderful. So I can take it that we'll have no more ineffectual encounters, right?"

Cocking his head to one side, he stared up at the ceiling. "I don't see how a lesbian can try and give a man stick about his performance between the sheets."

Corrine flashed him her perfect Osmond-like choppers. "It'll be the 17th, 18th or 19th then. Denise believes it will help if you had some notice. Hopefully this will stop it, ah, how shall I put it — coming as such a shock to you," sweetly she continued to rankle.

"OK, 17th, 18th or 19th, great. Anything else?" he asked unconcerned.

"You said you liked blow jobs. I want to give you a blow job." Corrine's whisper was probably loud enough for most of the ward to hear. Heads turned.

"Can't this keep till I get back?"

"I'm only holding it," Corrine sulked. The whole of the ward heard that. More heads turned.

"What's the matter with you woman? It's my cock, all right. Now, fucking stop!" he said from the corner of his mouth, looking around the ward.

Slowly pulling her hand from beneath the blanket, Corrine stared into his eyes, saying seductively, "I'm going to give you the best blow job you've ever had."

Watching Corrine this fired-up, Denise should have felt jealous or annoyed, but she didn't. It turned her on. She hadn't the slightest doubt that Corrine meant every word.

"Steve, lie back, I want you to imagine you're having a really great blow job... Are you thinking about it?"

His expression changed, Denise figured he was.

"Is it good? The best you've ever had?"

Denise guessed it might be, there was a certain sparkle in his eyes.

"Good. Now hold that thought. I'm going to top that. I..."

If he hadn't crossed his hands on his lap neither of them would have noticed. But he did. What was it the lads in the Para's called it? A tent pole?

"It's getting hard, isn't it?" Corrine exclaimed.

"Jeeeez, woman, I don't think they heard you in Scotland," he hissed.

Denise couldn't help it, she buried her face in her hands and laughed.

"Get off."

"I'm only holding it."

"I said, let go," he said with false calmness.

"It's getting even harder... Sticky," Corrine mused.

Taking a deep breath he slowly said, "Corrine, it's not made of wood, so please let go."

"See, I can do it." Corrine beamed across at her.

"Woman, trust me, you don't cop hold that hard. And I'm not letting your teeth anywhere near."

If she laughed any harder, she was going to fall off her chair. The tears were flowing down her cheeks and that nurse was back, giving them a librarian's disapproving looks.

"Do I have to to tell you again? Let go."

"You were thinking of the best blow job ever, weren't you? You really do like them, don't you?"

"I'm fucking serious now... Corrine, I mean it. Let fucking go!"

"But..."

"Corrine, everybody is looking," was all Denise could manage through the laughter.

Looking round the ward, Corrine embarrassedly pulled her hand out from under the blanket.

"I think it's about time we went." Still laughing,

Denise said from rather selfish motives; eager to get her HB home and into bed.

"That's right, ladies," he said folding his arms sulkily, "sod off and leave me with a stiffy that I can't do anything about?"

Corrine turned and gave him a, 'I'm going to fuck your fucking brains out', stare. "Get well, then get home, Steve. Then we'll see about that stiffy." It was almost a threat, said like she would have done to a woman.

Impatient to get home, Denise hoped that Merlene wasn't going to leave the scene altogether.

twelve

It sounded like Long John Silver coming up the stairs. She went to open the door.

"Couple of days in hospital before they toss you out on your ear," he grinned.

Following him as he manoeuvred on crutches down the corridor, she said, "We would have collected you."

"Thanks, but that's all right. Spent most of the day waiting round for the consultant to give me the all clear." He hobbled into his room and carefully sat on the bed with his leg outstretched.

"So, what have they said?"

"Not a lot," he shrugged. "Not a lot they can do, except set the knee and wait for it to mend. That's why they discharged me. Still talking bollocks about me never playing football though."

D"When will you be able to go back to *work?*" she asked poignantly.

"Don't know, couple of weeks, I suppose. Maybe even sooner."

"Would you like a tea or coffee?"

"No thanks."

"Is there anything I can get you?"

"No, I'm fine."

He seemed much more relaxed than when he was in the hospital.

"Corrine, stop looking at me like that."

She was about to protest.

"Stop looking at me like I was some task or mission to be accomplished. OK?" Adding a smile, he took the sting out of his statement.

"I don't think of you as a task or a mission, more a challenge."

Raising his eyebrows, he grinned then replied, "I'm the man, you're the lesbian, it's supposed to be the other way round."

"Well, I find it difficult to look at you without thinking about blow jobs," she teased.

He smiled at her a while before saying, "Let's just forget about blow jobs, shall we? They're not all they're cracked up to be."

"But you said you liked them."

"Nothing special. I can take them or leave them," he shrugged.

"I don't believe you."

"You don't have to believe me. Anyway, a blow job is just a quick way of getting the measure of a woman. That's why I suggested it."

This was doubly intriguing. "What do you mean?"

"Some women say, 'I'll give you a blow job, but don't think I'm gonna let you have sex with me'. Others will let you fuck them in all manner of ways, but a blow job is definitely out of the question."

Did this mean that some women had a blow job hang-up? She had an excuse, what was theirs? He continued while she considered this.

"The fact of the matter is; some women give blow jobs, and others don't. And I figured, quite rightly, that you wouldn't."

"You mean that you really don't mind whether I give you a blow job or not?"

"That's exactly what I mean. I didn't expect you to. I knew you wouldn't want to and was just trying to put you off."

There was no hiding her relief when he said he wasn't serious. Yes, he was a man and she a lesbian, but she wasn't exactly inexperienced — she could definitely show him a thing or two.

"By the way, you're doing it again." He gave her a cordial toothy smile then said, "Man and woman don't normally sit and talk about things like this."

"It sounds to me as if they should."

"OK. As we're talking about these things, what's a dental dam and what the hell do you use latex gloves for?"

She could feel herself redden.

"There was some pamphlet on the table in the front

room." He waved vaguely towards the door. "Something about health issues for dykes." Suddenly straightening in alarm, he hastily said, "I'm not calling you a dyke, it said dykes on the paper."

"They're used for safer sex."

Rolling his eyes upwards he pondered aloud. "Safer sex? I could make a guess at the gloves, but I'd probably get it wrong. As for the dental dams, the only thing I could come up with is 'gumshield'. And try as hard as I might, I can't figure out how and why you would use gumshields. Are dental dams and latex gloves an S&M thing?"

"No, they're for protection against AIDS." Why in God's name was she so flustered?

"When you made me have that test, they gave me a leaflet which was kinda interesting. Like, I didn't know you could get AIDS from using somebody else's razor or toothbrush. But nowhere did it say anything about muff diving. How do latex gloves protect your hand against AIDS? What can a woman do with her hand that a man can't?" He then stared her dead in the eye. "Are you into some weird things I've never heard about?"

Taking a slight breath, she gave him the explanation. "The gloves protect you and your partner when fingering."

He was now pulling a typical heterosexual puzzled frown, so she added. "Intravenous drug use is one way a lesbian can become infected."

He seemed satisfied and slightly relieved with that. "What about the dental dam?"

This was utterly ridiculous, she was now perspiring. "It's like a condom for your tongue. You use it when you are tonguing out someone's arse." No point in beating about the bush.

He shuddered as he seemed to form a mental picture. Folding his arms, he was again thoughtful, then, forming a slight smile, he stared her in the eye. "I see."

She decided to buy time. "Aren't you into anal sex?"

"No. Ain't into anything like that. In the army they used to call me The Missionary. I mean, if you like the woman — have respect for her — why would you want to treat her like some old trout? If the woman's got a sweet pussy, why would you want to stick your cock up her arse?"

"Come on, you must like something?"

He shook his head. "Me pon top, she pon top, doggy, that's it."

"But you must…"

"Don't start. Me and Andy used to argue this day and night. I know what I like," he said prodding himself in the chest. "I know what I don't like," he prodded again. "Hear what I'm saying?"

That's interesting. It might explain… "How many women have you had sex with?"

He gave her one of his cutting sideways glances. "More than you, a lot more than you. You don't believe me, do you?" Shaking his head, he stared out the window.

"No, I don't. I've slept with over forty women. OK?"

"This is definitely like chatting to a bloke," he said nodding to himself. "And I suppose, if I said I stopped counting after I passed a hundred and twenty, you'd say I was being big-headed, wouldn't you?"

"A hundred and twenty? Fuck off."

He simply turned to her and kissed his teeth, like Denise sometimes did.

"Steve, if you'd slept with that many, you'd know a lot more about women than you do."

"How do you know how much I know about women?"

"Because you've been with me." Perhaps she shouldn't have said that.

"Yeah." He was back to looking out the window.

"Steve, I didn't mean…"

"Don't worry about it. Because this is the — what do you call it — the kernel of the problem."

"What do you mean?"

"After I explain this, can we drop the subject?" He was still looking out the window.

"OK."

"Well, after screwing 'x' amount of women, you start to think to yourself, 'that's all well and good, but there's got to be more to it'. So you start to set standards. Standards like, when you're done, you want to have to peel her off the ceiling." Slowly he turned to her, a rueful expression on his face. "I know, despite all that I know, I'll never be able to do that to or with you. All right?"

She wasn't religious but that hit with the force of a divine revelation. Now she had to concede that although she finally felt she understood, she wasn't able to truly empathise. Steve believed that his powers of lovemaking were failing/deserting him. If she enjoyed the sex, then he was still a good lover. If she didn't, he wasn't.

"Steve, I'll show you exactly what to do to get me on the ceiling," she said with neophyte passion.

Folding his arms, he sarcastically said, "You planning on drawing me diagrams?"

Obviously she'd hit a nerve.

"No. I think we should spend a night together. By the morning…" She left that up to his imagination.

Shaking his head, he kissed his teeth again.

Being careful to avoid his leg, she crawled down the bed to him. Kneeling she took him in her arms and gave him a face-full of breast. "Steve, I'll be so sexy you won't have any more problems getting a hard-on."

"Sure," was his muffled reply.

It was a pity that she was wearing jeans and not a skirt. Even so she put one leg over his thighs and sat lightly in his lap. "I want you to have to peel me off the ceiling." She kissed him.

He broke the kiss, looked at her blankly for a while then he said, "Yeah, great. Now get off me."

She didn't move. "How many men do you think it takes to peel a full-on-dyke off the ceiling? But I'm going to teach you how to do it on your own. Imagine how good you'llbe then. I'm positively looking forward to it."

She started kissing him again. Slowly breaking the embrace he said, "Let's save it for the day."

"No, let's save it for a whole night."

"Whatever."

He looked as if he expected her to get off him, so she stayed put. "Over a hundred and twenty, eh?"

"Quite easy if you always go places you're never going back to. You can say and do anything — no comeback."

"In the army?"

"Army, football tours, whatever," he shrugged. "Was never into going and getting pissed with the lads. Not when there were better things to do."

"Kiss me again."

He did.

This time she broke the kiss, took off her glasses, folded them, and placed them on the side. Slowly climbing off him, she started to unbutton her jeans. Slipping them down she stepped out of her shoes then took off her knickers and pulled her rugby shirt off over her head.

"No. My leg is killing me," he said matter-of-factly. "Corrine, I'm not well. Corrine, ahh, look..."

Gently forcing him to lie on his back, she made sure he was comfortable and pulled his tracksuit bottom and boxers down his thighs. He didn't have a hard-on, but she didn't expect him to. Climbing back on him, she placed his penis flat against his tummy and started rubbing her fanny along it.

"Undo my bra."

With a fixed expression of disapproval and defiance he stared up at her.

"Do it."

His expression didn't change but he reached behind her with one hand and she felt the bra loosen. _Interesting._ She'd met women who had more difficulty undoing bras.

Their tongues were entwined, her hands around his neck, her firm nipples pressed tight against his chest, she was energetic and resolute. Tightening her grip, she felt damp as she rubbed up and down the shaft of his penis which had stiffened considerably. And he was moving in sync with her. Excellent, she knew she could do this. Sliding to the end she let it slowly penetrate her. She lost the sensation. Moving from side to side and back and forth she rode him. Changing tempo, sitting upright, lying forward, partial penetration, maximum penetration, no, it had definitely gone. She kept at this for a while then eased off him and went back to rubbing against penis.

That's more like it. Sensing a couple of minor tremors, she wondered if she was going to come. Then she knew she would. She became more deliberate and controlled in her movements. Feeling her fervour building she luxuriated. She held him even tighter.

"Ummm." Whipping his lips away from hers, he panted, "Stop."

Stop? She couldn't stop even if she wanted to. "Ahhhhhh..."

Opening her eyes, she saw that he was staring up at her, looking really cross. "Men don't like women who fake it, you know."

"I didn't fake it." She hadn't. She was wringing wet. And when she looked down she realised semen was smeared all over her stomach and breasts.

"What a disgusting mess," she screamed down at him. "You... You!"

Grabbing her glasses, she darted out of the room. In the bathroom she couldn't get the shower on fast enough.

***

All the way there he kept his mind blank. This wasn't one to plan out, he was in just the mood to wing it. By the time he arrived he would almost go as far as saying that he was feeling happy. In paying the fare, he made sure he took every penny of change. Not a penny tip.

Any driver how would just sit there and watch a man on crutches struggling get into his cab without offering help was lucky to be paid at all.

He made it to the gate, no problem. The lights were on. Good, she was home. Now for the stairs, one at a time, right up to the front door, no problem. Balancing on his good leg he pressed the bell and waited. To his right the curtains parted and her face appeared. She stared at him for a while then mouthed, 'Fuck off... Wanker'. The curtains swished closed in his face. He kinda expected that. Jeeeeze. He hated fucking women... No, he fucking hated women. Right, bitch. 'Fuck off'? We'll see about that!

To kick in a door you needed two serviceable feet, so that was out. Looking round he figured the porch to be about 10'x10'. More than enough room to get up a head of steam. Plus it would be all the more satisfying. Just like in the army he had a walk through first - hop, hop, hop, hop... pat-the-door. Then a dry run - hop, hop, hop, hop... nudge-the-door.

Right, door, you're coming off your fucking hinges. Hop, hop, hop, hop...

He was a bloke, more than capable of looking after himself. But one of the first things you do when you start to live with a woman is to check out her safety. Bolts, re-enforcing strips, double locks, no bastard was going to break in and rape his woman.

Suddenly he remembered this.

...Bang!

He bounced off. Hop... hop... hop, hop, hop, hop, hop - "Uuaaaaagh!" - backwards, head first, down the steps.

thirteen

Steve was stark bollock naked on the edge of the bath trying to balance and wash himself at the same time, when Denise came home. She rinsed and soaped a flannel. "I never did find out where you're ticklish. Where are you ticklish?" she casually asked over her shoulder.

"I'm not ticklish," came his tightly restrained answer.

"Really? Good. Let's do under the arms then."

Busily she washed under his arms and lower back, then conversationally threw in, "You've kept yourself in good nick. Corrine thinks your body is too hard and angular — no gentle curves or soft spaces. Plus, she can't stand designer stubble."

"Shave your pussy and she'll get used to it," he snapped.

"You think so?" She pretended to consider this. "*She* did that once, I didn't like it."

He regarded her with a level gaze before saying, "Denise, I don't know what you think you're doing, or why you're doing it, but you can do me a big favour."

She couldn't help having a quick look down to see if he had one of his instantaneous hard-ons. "A favour? What favour?"

He almost smiled. "She's your girlfriend, right? So tell her from me — endex."

"Endex?"

"End-of-the-exercise, over, finish, done. Find yourselves some other guy."

Not again! Men behaved irrationally when they couldn't perform. Well, if Corrine didn't know how to handle him… *Corrine, the things I do for you.* Deliberately staring at his cock she said, "Yes, I did get out of your bed to spite you the night you came back into my life. But I had to leave then or I'd never want to leave. Now, I'm not only jealous of you sleeping with my girlfriend, it's also… Well, she's getting something from you that I'm missing."

"Excuse me?"

Slipping her hand between his and taking hold of his balls, she said, "What? You don't think I miss it?"

He just cut his eye and sucked his teeth.

"Stan'up, man. Get 'pon yuh foot."

He didn't move.

Tossing the flannel behind her and stepping over to straddle his outstretched leg, she looked down at him. "One thing. Corrine must never know."

Shaking his head stoically, he stared back up at her but didn't move.

She gazed into his eyes. "Steve, I need you to stand. I want you to take me from behind. You know I like it like that."

He still didn't move.

"What do you want me to do, beg?"

"Denise, please leave me alone," he said reasonably.

"No. I'm not going to leave you alone. I want you to fuck me."

Laughing he said, "You can't pull a stroke like this, twice."

Releasing him, she stepped back, hitched up her dress, peeled off her knickers and gave him a face-full. "I'm talking this. It sweet. Yuh nuh want it?"

"Denise, I'm going to say this once more. Please leave me alone." Delivered calmly and patiently.

"Your mouth is saying one thing, but that…" she pointed to his fully erect penis, "…is saying something different."

Closing his eyes he shook his head. "Oh lawd, deliver me from mad women."

Grabbing him under the armpits, she started to tug. "Get yuh raas up and fuck me."

"It's OK, coz I know I'm going to wake up in a minute," he said with resignation, then, with her help, stood up.

Supporting him across the width of the bathroom she said, "You don't know how badly I need this, but…" she prodded him in the chest, "…shut your mouth to

Corrine."

"All right," he shrugged as if he wasn't taking any of this seriously.

She released him. "Remember I ain't as delicate as I look, hear what I'm saying?" *Men love hearing that you want them to fuck you as hard as they can.* Pulling up her dress she bent over the sink, exposing her arse, and grabbed hold of the taps.

"You're too short, I can't bend my leg." He sounded like he was trying not to laugh.

"Stay right deh." She flew out of the bathroom, into the bedroom, found her highest heeled stilettoes, then flew back to the sink and its taps. "OK? Now, hard and strong."

She didn't hate men. Nor did she 'hate' sex with them. But as she felt his cock slowly penetrate, she remembered — something essential was always missing.

She heard a door slam and someone coming up the stairs, the someone being Corrine. The shock made Denise panic. As she twisted in her high shoes, she grabbed Steve and, entwined, they crashed to the floor.

"Oh jeeeze! My knee, my knee, my knee!"

Heaving herself up, she kicked off her shoes, crawled over, grabbed her knickers and stuffed them into a shoe. Shoes in hand she stood, checked her hair in the mirror — *it'll have to do* — and turned to make a quick exit. He was using the side of the bath to try and haul himself back to his feet, she wanted to help but there wasn't enough time.

Quietly but firmly closing the door behind her, she ran on tiptoes to the bedroom. From the door, she threw the shoes under the bed. She heard him fall, but was only concerned about Corrine. Running across the corridor, she dived into the front room and slid on her knees to stop in front of the TV. She said a silent prayer that Corrine wouldn't slip her hand up her dress, which was her usual greeting.

"Hi, babes." Standing in the doorway, Corrine smiled down at her.

Legs curled under her she held out her hands in greeting. "Hi, Honey."

Slinking, Corrine started over. *Please God…*

"Denise. Denise!" he cried out. "Call an ambulance."

Corrine was already by the phone. Thank goodness, she hadn't noticed anything.

***

He hadn't bought Denise's 'I'm missing cock' line — that was simply bollocks. She was a woman who, if she wanted some wood, wouldn't have to look too hard, too far, or for too long. So, she'd given him the big come on for some other reason.

One thing about being doped-up to the eyeballs, your memory starts to play tricks. He was fairly sure that a couple of days had passed. He knew he'd been taken to another part of the hospital for an MRI scan, then back here for the operation, ending up in the same ward, though not the same bed. He recalled a detailed conversation with a doctor about both knees. He'd cocked-up the work they'd done on his right, so they were going to have to reset it. But it was his left knee that they found interesting with tendons, ligament and cartilage kaput! Lots of questions about the sports he played; how much and how often. Apparently, this sort of thing was common — an injury to one limb putting strain on the other, which aggravates an old injury. The Doc put it something along the lines of, 'It could have happened anytime; even from just squatting'. So, there you are, bending down to pick up something and your knee suddenly explodes. He thought that unlikely. Far more plausible was that every sexual encounter should carry a health warning.

On other matters his recollection was more ropey. More visits from his Mum and Dad, Andy, Naheed, Corrine and Denise were all a blur. In fact, he wasn't sure if he hadn't dreamt some of it. The Andy bit had definitely happened, there was obligatory gardening book with another little surprise inside. The Mum and Dad visit must have happened too, because there were the gungoo peas. But what about Tracy — the bitch. Had she really visited? Had she stood over his bed laughing her head off with her new boyfriend? He hoped that was only a nightmare.

fourteen

"How you doin', darling?"

"Uh?" Coming awake with a start, he saw Naheed smiling down at him.

Leaning down, her tits dying to jump out of her top, she planted a gorgeous kiss on his lips. The guy opposite, whose name he'd learnt was Gordon, was giving him the 'You lucky, lucky, lucky, bastard', look.

"All of a sudden, I'm much better."

"So, they're lesbians."

"Er…?"

"The girls you live with," she said, sitting down gracefully.

"Er… yeah…?"

"The two of them were hovering and I didn't know who they were…"

He had no recollection of Naheed, Corrine and Denise being there at the same time. What else had occurred?

"It was really odd, we just sat there looking at each other. You know, like in one of those films where you get three women sitting around the man's death bed who have just found out that they are all his wives." Laughing, she continued, "Want to know what I thought? It looked to me like the white girl was your girlfriend. She'd come to see you with her best friend. Now, from her best friend's body language, she suddenly realised that there was something going on between you two as well. And of course, they both wanted to know my relationship with you."

"You like romance fiction, do you?"

"Very funny. I'm more than enough for any man."

He grinned back. Now he had some understanding of what has transpired, he was no longer worried.

"By the way, what's a gimpy?"

"A what?"

"A gimpy. You were muttering something in your sleep about, 'Cocking a gimpy in Milan'."

"Was I?" He laughed.

"Yes you were. Is it some Italian dish, if you know what I mean."

"You sure I said that? It's what they called the G.P.M.G in the army," he said matter-of-factly. "General Purpose Machine Gun."

"Yeah, right!"

"You expect me to believe you were fantasizing about a machine gun? More like some Italian slag, right? What did you do, share her?"

There were tears in his eyes. "Milan, is a type of

MAW. Medium Antitank Weapon."

"You were cocking it," she said, unbelievingly.

"You have to cock a gun before you fire it."

"Having dreams about women I could understand... but a machine gun, now that's weird."

Still laughing he turned to her, "Nothing weird about it, it makes perfect sense. Spent far more time on the gun than with women."

"Oh really?" she asked sarcastically.

"Yes really," he answered sweetly. "I was usually on the gun; probably because I'm tall. Give a big bloke the gimpy and from a distance it isn't obvious who's carrying the gun. The gun is most of a section's firepower. So, if you can spot the gunner, you shoot him first," he answered logically.

"That's exactly what I'll do, if you ever..."

Once or twice he'd received similar smiling threats from one woman or another. He hadn't taken them seriously then.

He pulled her towards him, muttering "You know I'm not like that." He'd seen 'nuff man running more than one woman and have it blow up in his face because one of the women found out about the other.

"If you're 'good to me' then there isn't anything another woman can do for you that I couldn't, or wouldn't, do..."

And if he wasn't 'good to her', she'd chop his dick off.

'Need to know' was a pretty standard military principle which, he'd always thought, civilians would do well to adopt. She didn't need to know his most erotic or exotic experience. Nor did he need to know hers. Too much man always try to talk themselves out of the mire and end up deeper in it. He could feel a smile forming as he pulled the sort of answer that came straight out of Andy's top drawer. "No other woman… other women…"

A dangerous look passed her eyes.

"…just kidding…"

"Those two les—"

"Denise and Corrine."

"I thought you had your own…"

"I do, this is just temporary." Naheed was looking like she expected him to say more so he continued, "I had to get out. And until we've… sorted it out, she's got the flat."

Making herself more comfortable on his bed, she then asked, "What caused it?"

"The split?"

"Yes."

Suddenly embarrassed, he shifted about. "Some geezer."

"Bitch!" Then she flung her arms round his neck.

Whatever else, it was great being pampered. "Better it happened now than three years from now. And anyway, every cloud has a silver lining, as they say."

Releasing his neck, she pulled back to stare into his eyes. "What do you mean?"

"Well, on one hand I've busted both my knees and been chucked out of my flat. But on the other, I've got you, babe."

She planted another dynamite kiss on his lips. When she eventually let go, she said, "Yes, you have. And I want to make love to you so badly it hurts... How about a BJ?"

He gulped when reminded of the last time.

"I think they're just about to start serving dinner."

"Are they?"

Her breast pressing firmly into his chest seemed to be interfering with his reasoning. Then to cap it all, she took his hand and thrust it up her miniskirt, she was knickerless. Oh God! With her hand busily rummaging under the sheet, it looked like another blow job was definitely on the cards.

"Yeah. Mind you, sometimes they're about five minutes late." He made sure he sounded suitably eager.

She smiled cheekily. "Five minutes? Not long enough. You can't rush a really good BJ." Quickly checking the clock, she added, "I'll get here fifteen minutes earlier tomorrow. OK?"

"OK. If I'm not here when you come, I'll be in the bathroom having an icy cold bath. In fact, I think I'll go have one as soon as I've eaten."

She got up, readying herself to leave. "I'll see you

tomorrow then babe..."

With that she vamped out, her knickerless perfect behind attracting stares, including envious ones from Alverna as she trolleyed in the ward's dinner. With his attention fixed on Naheed, he hadn't noticed Alverna going about her business. She'd glanced at him though, for a split second, a glance that said 'whatever your numerous women can do, I can do better'. He recognised a challenge when he saw one but this was just the final block of a very confusing jigsaw. Because there was no way he was even going to think about it, about Alverna or about anyone else for that matter. No way. He had Naheed and he was going to be good to her, really, really good to her, the best good he'd ever been. Endex. It's just that he still had one minor task to perform: he had a baby to father.

fifteen

She'd been pretty pissed but not so pissed that she wasn't pissed off. She was just waiting for her to start. If Denise said one word, just one word, out of line then...

But there she was, sat in silence in this All Bar One for a heart to heart, a public place, a neutral place so that they could take stock, clear the air and all that.

"Why are you looking so cross,?"

"Am I? I'm not cross, just lost in thought." Half turning, Denise gave one of her cutting glances.

Both had worried about the other inadvertently uncovering what had become secrets. Both sensed that something was amiss. Both could sense the other's recent sexual encounters but both wanted the other to be the first to accuse. Neither would commit herself. Let her who is without sin...

"I mean," said Corrine, her stomach for verbal confrontation suddenly gone, "of all the things we could argue about... I mean, Steven?"

The corner of Denise's mouth twisted into a smile.

Corrine pressed on. "Do you think he has come between us?"

"Come between us?"

She tutted. "Especially as it's you he fancies."

"He doesn't fancy me," Denise protested.

"How can you say that?"

"Corrine, that was when he was eighteen... I suppose this thing has put certain stresses and strains on our relationship. You know what? I think you're pretty amazing to have taken it this far."

Corrine was taken aback. The last thing she expected was reconciliation before they'd even had the war.

"You are. I mean it."

"But...?"

"No but... If we want this baby, you have to be the one to have it... I know that. I just lost it, got a bit jealous... It's a sign of how I feel. Isn't it?"

"But I'm still not pregnant." Corrine said despondently.

"That doesn't stop you being amazing."

Denise leaned over to her lover and whispered something in her ear. Soon after, they went home and to bed for some fantastic sex.

***

She suspected that sex was always better when she was slightly drunk because she was more relaxed.

She awoke clear-headed, satiated, feeling alive and

just, well, happy. While she busied herself for work, she told Corrine it was OK if she no longer wanted to have the baby, as long as they were together then everything was fine; if Steve was the problem, then that was also fine, they'd just find someone else; if Corrine was no longer certain and wanted to wait, no problem; whatever the reason, she didn't care as long as Corrine was happy.

Corrine took this in but didn't say anything for a while. "I'm far too young for my biological clock to be going haywire. So me getting all broody must have something to do with you."

Denise stopped what she was doing (applying her make-up) to consider this. This was the first time Corrine had actually professed to feeling broody. *She* was making Corrine broody? Corrine must have seen her confusion because she added, "I'd never even thought about having children until I met you."

After Denise had left for work, Corrine confronted Steve with the good news.

"Denise and I are going to be life partners."

"Congratulations," he sounded sincere, if sleepy. "When's the big day?"

"We haven't set a date," Corrine continued. "However, because we are going to be life partners, we would like to have one more attempt."

"Just one more and then we knock it on the head?" he yawned, checking his understanding. "Because you are 'tying the knot'?"

"Yes," Corrine admitted.

Raising his eyebrows he said, "I'm easy, so whatever. But why?"

"Because we love each other and would like to have a child by you."

"OK." He nodded to himself. "Now, stupid question, but what happens if you get divorced, or whatever you call it?"

Corrine seemed perplexed. "Why is this an issue now?"

"It's not an issue now." He shrugged. "It's just that I never thought about it before."

"That isn't your concern," she answered emphatically.

As if thinking aloud he said, "You want me to father a child but what happens to it isn't my concern. Interesting."

"Thousands of men…"

"Corrine, I'm not giving you a hard time. Just listen. Right? As the baby father, I'm one of your life partners, so when you and Denise take your vows, I want you also to promise that you're never going to get divorced and that you will both always be there for the child. Then I'm cool."

"All right. I'll speak to Denise when she gets home."

***

"As this is the last time, I'm going to make it rather special."

He told himself that he was probably reading too much into that statement. He'd never been inside a Turkish brothel but he figured the way theu'd transformed the inside of their bedroom was how one would be: lots of candles but, with the curtains drawn, the room was still dark; a mixture of several aromas; soft 'mood music' emanated from somewhere.

Corrine was standing by the window, arms by her sides, wearing a long dark dressing gown and an equally silly grin, trying to be cool, sexy and inviting, waiting for something.

He hadn't noticed the champagne because he was trying to get to grips with being inside this subdued Middle Eastern den. Walking up to him she held out a glass and as he reached for it she bent to kiss him. She didn't just kiss him, she stuck her tongue, in a 'let's get it on' sort of way, into his mouth.

"Cheers," he smiled, when she was through, and clinked glasses.

She said thoughtfully, "I think I could enjoy sex with you if you shaved."

He hadn't shaved in days

"This is the last time, right?"

Corrine nodded.

"So we want to make it special for both of us, right?" Again she nodded but this time smiling with pleasure. "I'm a man, men grow beards." He shrugged.

"Not all men. Amerindians don't have beards."

He'd never heard of that but, come to think of it, when was the last time you saw an Indian with a beard in a cowboy film?

She wriggled out of the dressing gown; underneath she was wearing black knickers. Standing there in all her glory, eyes slightly unfocused, she smiled warmly down at him. His dick poked out from under his Arsenal away strip top. Placing a hand on his shoulder, she pushed him down and, careful of his knees, climbed on top to sit across his stomach.

"Steve, what's the maximum number of times you've made love to a woman in one night?"

He knew the answer, it was six. But he also knew it had little to do with him — there were just some women who could bring that out on a man. "Dunno, three maybe four times. You?"

"About the same, then I start to get sore."

Now there's a thought. What did lezzies do…? No. He wasn't going to even think about it. "Why did you ask?"

She gave him a spaced-out grin. "So, four it is then." Four times? It would be a long night.

"Aren't you going to blow out the candles?"

"No," he said, "not yet."

sixteen

"Are you ready to come yet?"

"You know what, I've worked out how to 'stan 'pon it all night'. Just get the woman to keep asking," he changed his voice to be girlish, "Are you ready to come?"

She kept up this blow by blow account like she felt she had to explain what was going on: "This is really uncomfortable." "This isn't too bad. Do they enjoy this, the women you've slept with?" "I think I should go faster." "No. I'll never achieve an orgasm like this." "If I raise myself slightly, like this, is that better?" "You've just ejaculated, haven't you? How long will it take you to get another hard-on?" And so it went, all bloody night.

From the way she was carrying on, you'd think they were trying every position in the Kama Sutra when all that was happening was he was lying on his back with her on top. It should have been, at best, distracting; at worst, off-putting. But he just laid back and took it in.

Why? Because whatever she'd taken had put her in randy mode, and what's the point of slowly and sensuously running your tongue round a woman's nipples if she wasn't getting off on it? Then there was her cold-blooded determination to have an orgasm. Even he had come to accept that she was, as they would say, 'a full-on dyke', so an orgasm was hardly likely. But no. She was like a dog with a bone, she was going to have an orgasm if it killed her. She set about using his cock like a dildo, even pointing out the 'inconvenience' of it being attached to the rest of him.

"I just know I'm going to get pregnant," she gasped.

Great. He hoped so. Then all he had to do was get better and get on with his life with Naheed.

***

Life's a bitch, you marry one, and then you die. When this statement begins to make some sense, that's when you can tell that you've grown up, or more accurately, you are expected to act like a grownup. He laughed to himself. He didn't suppose that many people could pinpoint the exact time and place that they grew up. He could and with some precision — 3:37 am, Monday 21 September, Southampton General Hospital.

Never being one to hang out with the lads (all they did was get pissed, made asses of themselves and cramped your style), plus around Aldershot there were too many Squaddies joints, with too many tarts and too many crap hats. He and Andy used to go further afield. Aldershot to Southampton in less than an hour. Lots of students, great nightlife, loads of available women. So it made a degree of sense that after they left the army they went to chill out in their home-from-home, Southampton.

Mind you, by then, Katrina (slag!) was pussy-whipping Andy into moving back to London to shack up with her. Of course, Andy didn't see it that way, but to an outsider it was obvious: he had been ambushed by some well thought-out, seriously elaborate, pussy-science. Steve suspected that once she'd captured him, Katrina put him on half rations and, then, only if he was a good boy; the month had an R in it; she hadn't broken a fingernail recently; and they'd stopped burning down the rain forest.

Having sorted a job and temporary accommodation, Steve went solo in Southampton, fine-tuning and developing his woman skills. Things like: _When you get her back to your place, don't try and get her drunk, instead get her to take her shoes off. Because when a woman takes her shoes off, she's always reluctant to put them on again._

Then one day an idea came out of nowhere and he created his masterpiece 'tequila tape' (because it did the job of a bottle of tequila). Sixty minutes of seamless music per side (not that he ever needed more than one side). Every track hand-picked with loving care; ten minutes of loud pumping dance — sit opposite and chat about life the universe and anything she wants to talk about (she expected you to have tried it on by now); a gradual change to twenty minutes of more soulful music — stay where you are, the conversation moves on to feelings and girly things like that; smooth change down to twenty minutes of bump and grind music, get up, fix her a drink, when you sit back down, you're next to her (by now she'd have taken off her shoes), the conversation now about your feelings for her. Seamless! Which way is the bed please?

Somewhere in all this fun he met Rebecca. She'd just finished her degree and wasn't in a hurry to go home to Derbyshire. It was fantastic at first, then she started mirroring Katrina's behaviour. He told her nicely. She didn't listen. Next he was more 'in your face'. She didn't listen. So he told her to wind her fucking neck in. She still didn't listen! Then he told her he was moving back to London, the woman seemed to expect that he'd want her to come with him. She took it badly when she found out otherwise.

In the middle of the night he got a phone call from her flatmate to say Rebecca had taken an overdose. He got there as quickly as he could. At 3:37 am on Monday the 21st of September he walked into Emergency, just in time to hear her getting her stomach pumped. It was a pretty distressing sound, one that would haunt him for as long as he lived. In the end he found out that she was never on the point of dying. He swore that night that he'd stay well away from headcases. But how the fuck do you know before it's too late?

About six months after coming back to London Tracy crossed his path. She was serious about netball, he was serious about football — they hit it off like a house on fire. Because he'd turned over a new leaf, instead of just shagging her and getting on with business, he asked her to move in. On the morning she was due to move in, his final act of maturity was to take his tequila tape and chuck it in the dustbin.

Pussy till it was coming out your ears when they are after you. They get you and move in; suddenly it dries up. He wasn't too bothered, he sort of expected it — he just got on with grown-up man things like working hard to earn the money to give her the things that she said she wanted. Just when he'd made the adjustment to living with Tracy even more grown-up stuff was called for. With Andy in Jamaica, Katrina, and her unbelievable body, chose that moment to make her move. But hey, was he a grown-up or was he a grown-up? He dealt with it and kept his dick in his pants. So his best mate's woman got the real ache because he wouldn't fuck her. Life!

On reflection he should have told Andy as soon as he set foot back in England, but Katrina (crazy bitch) threatened to go crying to Andy saying he'd tried it on her!

Katrina was Andy's woman, she was his problem.
And anyway, he was starting to have problems of his
own — Tracy.

Yes, she was the clever one. Yes, she always won the
arguments. But, he was always one step ahead of her.
You suss that your woman has started to take the piss
and is shagging someone else (this is after you've been
strictly — despite the temptations — monogamous,
proof that God has a sense of humour). What do you
do? You could put yourself back into circulation. Or you
could bring things tidily and painlessly to an end. This
was what he tried to do but it didn't work out that way.
He wasn't angry, he wasn't even slightly annoyed, if
anything, his only concern was getting back his flat.
Though he was a little sad that he hadn't dumped his
tequila tape over a more worthy woman...

seventeen

He slept, more like passed out. When he came to, Marti was standing over him dangling house keys.

"Hi Steve… I'll be taking care of you today," said Marti breezily.

She was wearing a maroon velvet trouser suit and still looking well criss, definitely in 'game' mode. He wasn't, he was far too tired.

"Didn't expect to see you so soon. So how you doin'?"

"I'm fine, how are you?" That she delivered in a 'let battle commence' tone.

"I'm good."

"Are we going to dance around each other or are we going to get down to business?"

"Business? Whatever do you mean?"

"Least we forget, you promised to amaze me with what a boy can do. Put up or shut up."

She gave him a 'Ready?' smile, sat back and slowly eased herself out of her jacket. Underneath she was wearing an 'almost' see-through white blouse and no bra. "Remember the cans? That's, how shall I put it, the minimum standard. So, big boy, dazzle me."

She might as well have said, 'gwan nuh, if yuh t'ink yuh bad, teck it'. That's what she meant!

Indisputable fact: when stark bollock naked, women do not look as sweet as when partially dressed. Indisputable fact: Marti; woman; stark bollock naked; as she took the half a pace from the chair to his bed, looked... looked, well... raaaas!

She didn't say anything, she didn't need to — she just looked down and laughed in his face.

This is fucking war now, man! "Come," he patted the bed, "Sit closer. Let's see what uncle Steve's got for you."

She sat close enough for him get a whiff of that subtle smell of roses but far enough away so that he had to reach if he wanted to touch. And those tits... Oh God! He was going to start to drooling again.

"You don't have to rush off anywhere, do you?" he asked. "Good because this will take some time. Let's see now, where do we start? Top down or bottom up?" Obviously this was a bottom up then a top down job. You couldn't get to be even an apprentice pussy mechanic unless you understood that fingers, thumb and tongue were part of every pussy mechanic's repertoire.

"Nice feet, great legs. Pass one this way," he

suggested.

Give the lady credit! She didn't cross her arms or legs, she just sat there in a 'do what you will' pose.

Despite what they said in his favourite film of all time, in his experience, the feet weren't the place to start. To get the ball rolling, you want to start with the back of the knees and the inner and outer thighs. Taking her by the ankles, watching her slowly slide down the wall, he gently pulled her down to him.

Nice!

Now then, he couldn't play the piano but it must be a bit like this — gently stroking the keys until you hit the right chord. She didn't resist nor did she protest, instead she gave him an, 'Is this it?' look. To which he gave back a, 'Man, I ain't even started yet'. He was going to work-over the back of knees and thighs for a good ten minutes. Tilting her head to the side, she started staring at the ceiling in a, 'Oh, this is so boring' kinda of way.

He'd heard somewhere that orgasms were all mental. Mental or not, lesbian or not, he was going to play until he hit the spot. He went to work on her knees…

"That's ticklish." She jerked her leg away.

Ticklish my arse! Spot One. If you wanted to be really wicked, when you started playing with the thighs, especially the inner thighs, you could tease a woman to death with that. He could, but he wasn't going to, well, not yet. Woman, watch this move. Taking one of her legs, he placed it over his shoulder, his right shoulder, so that her legs were now wide apart giving him an eyeful of pussy. She looked at him but didn't say a word. Dropping a couple of rodent moves on the inner thigh, she quivered; Spot Two. Having got her undivided attention, he switched to stroking her outer thigh and arse. Man, this was fun!

She was still trying hard to look bored — trying, but not succeeding. Having to change position a bit because this was killing his back, with his free hand he reached for her neck and shoulder. This was more of a gentle massaging move. No hurry, no rush, nobody was going anyplace, he just kept it going. Surprise, surprise; Spot Three.

He must now have been a good fifteen minutes into some of his favourite party tricks. Taking her leg off his shoulder and placing it on the other side of him, so he was straddled between them, he leant forwards — like he was going for the pussy. *Naw!* He took his time, plenty of time, teasing the belly button, her manicured pubic hairline and otherwise in that general neck of the woods with his tongue. Do that to a woman and, if you do it right, she'll arch her back. Lesbian or no lesbian. Do it with style and she'll reach for the sky. Sweet smelling as it was, did this woman have any idea of how long it was going to be before he got to her pussy?

This is where the feet come in. Toes, ankles, calves; in that order and each being given its due care and attention; then back to the knee. *There! You see?* Just when, despite herself, she began to give off the 'this is rather nice' vibe, he got her reluctantly to turn over. Then stretching like buggery he worked the spine with his fingers, thumbs and tongue, from the top of her neck to her arse. He then brought into play her tits, but not the actual nipples themselves — that he was saving for later.

Just then she went sort of limp, like tension simply floated out of her body, and made a very relaxed 'Ahh' sound. Well there you go, so much for, 'I'm a lesbian, you cannot do it for me'.

She turned over, he didn't get her to do it, she did it all by herself and ended up lying exactly where she started. Narrowing her eyes she gave him a 'you bastard' look.

He wasn't done yet, though. *Oh, no.* Resting his chin on one hand, he slipped his other hand between her legs almost, but not quite, touching her pussy. Leaving it there, he sucked her tits gently. She gave him an 'attend to the pussy and leave my nipples alone' glare. Obviously, at some point, he was going to play with it, but that was still some time away.

Making like he was about to pray, he parted her legs and took his time placing a leg over each shoulder. He wouldn't go so far as to say that she got all eager, however, she did wiggle about to make it easier for him get her in a position where she wasn't lying on his legs but he could brush his chin with her pubes.

Eyes sparkling she gave him a 'got ya' smile. Very slowly, almost lazily, she reached up, put her hand behind his head, left it there for a bit (just so he'd know the score), then pulled his head down. *OK. OK.* 'Hello Mission Control, we have premature pussy engagement'. 'Roger that, you know what to do'. Yes! He certainly did. When all is said and done, there are only two types of pussy in the world; renk pussy and sweet pussy. This was sweet — damn sweet!

He went with the flow. No rush, no hurry, nice and steady. It wasn't too long before she started to wiggle and wind. A little more and she wiggled, wind and whine. Little more and she started them woman-type judders with their accompanying moans and groans. Now the woman was virtually sitting up with both hands around his head. Why? He knew what to do.

Egaging her pussy like a damn virtuoso, he waited, and waited, put his face on, waited some more and then... pulled away.

"Jesus, I could really do with a cup of tea."

The look on her face! If only he had had a camera. She did a double take, like she wasn't hearing right.

"I'm really parched. Are you thirsty? I could murder a tea," he repeated.

Eyes mere slits, she pulled a 'YOU FUCKING BASTARD!' face. For a moment he thought she was going to start shouting, but she controlled it. *Good girl.*

You know shouting at me would be an admission that you love dick too much. Whipping her leg over his head, deliberately ramming his ear with her knee in the process, she flashed a 'I'm going to kill you' glance and waltzed out of the room. "Two sugars," he called after her. Even when she is seriously fucked off, how can a woman still manage to look graceful and horny?

Hmm, definitely a black woman's arse.

How long had they been at this? About an hour he figured. He laughed to himself. 'I'm a full-on dyke, you're a man, there's no way you can make it play'. Yeah, _right!_ It just goes to show that if the man knows what he is doing, he can wring joy out of any pussy.

Strutting back in with a mug in her hand it was plain to see that she'd calmed down and was back in game mode. Handing over the mug, she gave him a pretty unconvincing 'I wasn't really that bothered' smile. Taking the mug with one hand, he patted the mattress with the other and returned a 'Yeah, _sure_' smile.

She had a thoughtful look at his dick like if she had a five-iron she'd tee-off on it. She knew what he'd done and she probably thought she knew why he'd done it.

He raised the mug to his lips. "You haven't spat in this or anything like that have you?"

Her response was a disdainful 'I wouldn't lower myself' head flick and turn away.

He took a sip, "Refresh my memory. What was the deal here? Was it that me, Mr Heterosexual, couldn't ring your, Ms Lesbian's, bell?"

She turned back to him. "Excuse me, Mr Heterosexual with the miniscule member, my bell isn't remotely close to being rung."

"I was just checking," he shrugged. Clearly he couldn't leave her too long otherwise she'd go off the boil. "Speaking of bells, shall we get back to it?"

She gave him a long, hard, questioning stare. Lips slowly drawing over her teeth, she seemed to come to some decision. Flinging a leg over his thighs she copped an 'I ain't afraid of you' attitude. Gulping a mouthful of tea and putting down the mug, he looked down at the leg like he felt it wasn't supposed to be over his thighs. Then he gave her a 'Are you sure you're up for this?' smile. Switching to combat mode, she eased back and flipped one leg and then the other over his shoulders.

OK then.

What he was about to do, he'd never quite done before — it was going to take some skill. But hey, 'Skilly' was his middle name. As soon as his tongue touched her clitoris, she started to gyrate. For the next five minutes or so he just kept it on the button. Hands back around his head, the lady was working up a severe head of steam. Then, just for a brief second, she paused to check what he was doing. Satisfied, she went for it in a big way:

One of those long, long, long, drawn out, 'Please, please, please don't stop'/'I want to scream the place down but I'm not going to'/'Oh God I can't stop quivering'/'It's going to simply take ages before I'm able to stand' orgasms.

Eventually (we're talking minutes here), she came down off the ceiling, flopped back on the bed and gave him a most gratifying and slightly dazed 'Bugger me, how did you manage that?' smirk.

It's great having a woman, long after the deed is done, still hot and trembling next to you. Now, you'd think a lesbian would know a move like that, wouldn't you? Pure skill! A mouthful of burning hot tea, tongue in and out of your mouth, without spilling a drop. He should christen that the 'The Hot Tongue Trick'. Wicked!

After a while she sat up and, stretching, reached for her jacket.

"What are you doing?"

Mid-motion she froze and stared at him, her eyes gleaming. "Getting the condoms. You told me to bring some, remember?"

He started to laugh. "Didn't I hear you insult Diablo by saying something about miniscule dicks?"

"Diablo?" She cracked up.

"Don't you women know nuffink? A man's got to name his tool, hasn't he?"

By now she had tears rolling down her cheeks. "Have I hurt its feelings?" she asked between gasps.

"Not half."

"Poor Diablo!"

Golden rule: always make them laugh.

Let's see now: Corrine yesterday; Marti today; and Naheed… Hmm, he was getting far too much of a good thing. *Something bad is going to happen and it's going to happen soon.* It had to. But he'd worry about that some other time.

He turned to her and smiled. "Yeah. Condoms. Good idea."

eighteen

They had their engagement dinner party to prepare. "You mean you're having another one of those 'six mad dykes' do's," Steve had said. "If it's all right with you, I'm gonna stay right out of it."

Babs was the first to arrive, two and a half hours early, looking rather upset.

"I need to have a word with Steve."

Corrine froze and stared at her. "Steve?"

Babs confirmed, "Yes, Steve."

Letting her in, Corrine suddenly had a bad feeling about this. "He's in his room. Call me nosy if you must, but why do you want to see him?"

"I need to check something."

Corrine rapped on Steve's door, opened it, nudged Babs through, followed her in and closed it behind her.

Book in hand Steve was sitting up in bed staring from one to the other with a perplexed 'what do you want?' look. Babs turned to her signifying that this was a private matter and that she should leave. She stayed put.

Eventually he asked, "Yeah?"

Babs took a shallow breath then asked, "Have you slept with Marti?"

His face sagged with disbelief. "What?"

"Have you had sex with Marti?"

With the same look of incredulity he turned to his landlady for support. "Corrine, what the fuck is she talking about?"

"Marti said that you have," Babs continued in the same emotionless drone.

"This is another wind-up, right?"

"Are you saying you haven't?" Babs didn't sound convinced, but she seemed relieved.

"You crazy?"

His look of total bewilderment and unquestionable innocence was an Oscar performance.

"She had sex with *someone*," Babs said flatly. "When I confronted her she confessed it was you."

Putting both hands to his head, as if he had a severe headache, he muttered, "Am I missing something here? Marti is a lesbian! What are you on about? And anyway, how can you tell she had sex with someone?"

"I can. She did. Was it you?"

"Babs, ah, I don't know what to say. I know this isn't funny, right? But I could just about cope with some geezer accusing me of shagging his bird. Do you know how weird what you're saying sounds? I'll say it one more time: I haven't had sex with Marti. OK?"

The fucking lying bastard!! Denise had slipepd into the room on hearing the commotion and was standing so close that Corrine could feel her breath on the back of her neck.

"Are you absolutely sure?" Babs pressed, his categorical denial had obviously thrown her.

"What do you mean, 'am I sure'?" His face finally cracked into a grin. "Trust me, I'd remember."

"OK. I had to ask," Babs answered distractedly. Clearly her thoughts were switching to other possibilities.

"Did she really put me in the frame?" He seemed genuinely interested.

"Yes, she did," Babs answered, now in 'So, who could it be then?' mode.

"Babs, want me to take a really wild, off the wall stab at this?" Without waiting for assent and looking thoughtful, he continued. "OK, here it is: a bloke is caught out so he owns up. Naturally his woman goes ballistic. Just when she's about to detonate, he explains that it was with another bloke. She freaks out and starts to lose it. Just as she is about to fall right over the edge, he goes, 'Only kidding, it was a woman'. All of a sudden him putting it about doesn't seem that bad. You get me?"

Seamless! How could he lie with such sincerity? The only other person that she knew who could lie with

such consummate ease was... Marti. Oh no! What had
she started?

Corrine took Babs by the arm and headed straight for
the kitchen and the bottles of wine. This was going to be
an interesting evening.

Just as she popped the cork the doorbell went. No
prizes for guessing who. Yep, the evening was certainly
taking shape. She paused for a moment then casually
opened the door.

"She's here, isn't she?" Marti seemed fairly relaxed.

"I told you to stop, didn't I?" She matched her for
layed-backness.

"So you did, darling. But these things do have a habit
of taking on a life of their own." Marti smiled girlishly.

"Yes, indeed they do." She mirrored the smile. "He's
denied it by the way, and she believes him. Now
sweetheart, before we go upstairs..."

"Yes, I know — don't spoil the evening."

"That goes without saying. I was about to suggest, or
perhaps even insist, that Denise... Well, need I say
more?"

"Understood. Here are your keys." Flashing her a
beaming smile, Marti gave them back to her.

Letting her in and following Marti up the stairs
Corrine wondered if there was a specific word for a
female rascal. Marti stopped dramatically at the kitchen
door and said, "It was a lie. It was the most hurtful thing
I could think of at the time. I'm very sorry."

She didn't quite hear Babs' response because the doorbell went again.

***

There was an impressive and satisfying collection of empty wine bottles by the time the party moved to the dining room. Denise felt sick and rushed to the bathroom. Corrine followed her.

Denise was stooping over the toilet basin. "I'll be all right," she said with a reassuring smile. "It's just that I keep feeling nauseous."

Corrine closed the door behind her and stared at Denise uncertainly.

"Stop worrying, I'll be fine." Whatever it was that Denise saw in Corrine's face caused her to turn from the toilet to face her. "What?" she asked puzzled.

No, not absurd at all. Opening the cabinet, Corrine reached in, took one out and offered it to Denise. Perplexed Denise's eyes went from Corrine to the packet in her hand to Corrine to the packet to Corrine to the packet and finally back to Corrine. It seemed to take Denise a ridiculous amount of time to grasp the significance of being handed a pregnancy test kit.

***

What do you do when you've been caught bang to rights? Come clean or lie through your teeth? Stupid

question. After they left, he went back to reading his
book. It was a good book (wars, mercenaries, beautiful
women, spaceships, knife missiles — it had everything),
but thinking about Naheed was distracting him.

A loud hysterical shriek came from somewhere. It
was the kind of ear-piercing noise a woman makes
when she sees a fucking huge rat and leaps onto a chair.
Sounds like the party's kicking off.

Moments later, the bedroom door flew open and one
blonde, 5'5" knife missile with an expression of focused
rage, followed by another blonde, 5'7" more curvaceous
knife missile, followed by a brunette 5'10" knife missile
with very red lips, streaked into the room. They zeroed
in on him. Corrine kicked him in the bollocks (he was
pretty sure she was aiming at his knee, but being a non-
footballer she missed). *Aaaaaaarggh!* He bent over
double. Then all three knife missiles were on top of him
raining down blows. *What the fuck's the matter with them?*

Now here's an interesting thing: women can't, or
don't know how to, punch. No one ever taught him how
to punch, but the last time he really belted someone (a
wooden top who was giving it a large, 'You'll never
mount guard at Buckingham Palace') the guy was
unconscious before he hit the deck. These women were
playing patter cake on him — more like closed hand
slaps. Not only that, they were all so intent on dishing
out some vengeance they were simply getting in each
other's way. *Women!* You can't help but love 'em.

So there he was, being mugged by three demented dykes. It should have been a 'no contest'. Should have been, but wasn't. Corrine, Marti and Babs were no match for him. As they laid into him they screeched but said nothing. They refused to give in though.

***

"Well?"

The 'I've just popped round to see how you were', was bollocks. Andy was on an night fishing expedition. "Well what?"

"Cho." Andy was pretending to be annoyed. "You saying you haven't been dealing with two lesbians then?"

"Is where you hear this?"

"Hear it? Bwoy, I almost felt it. I just went to see my sister, right. Talk about walking into a storm! You ever hear women chat 'bout castration and mean it?"

He tried not to laugh. "So they were a bit vexed?"

"Vex? You know how women stay from time. One man does something to them and it's a free for all 'pon any man dem come across. I couldn't stay in that place, it was not safe. I tell you, man, I was glad Jo was there."

Steve laughed then shrugged. "Shit happens."

Andy sat back and folded his hands. "Details."

"There's nothing to say." He mirrored him in folding hands.

"Details!"

"Look, they started it, right. I don't see what they have to bawl about."

Andy twitched and spied him through one eye. "She's pregnant, that's what they've got to bawl about."

"No, she fucking isn't! Well, she could be but she wouldn't know it yet."

"How come you so sure?" Andy wasn't sold. "Details."

"Business, business, just business."

He could see it in his eyes, Andy was not going to let the matter drop. He was just going to try another route. "So what happened between you and Katrina when I was in Jamaica?" he asked casually.

Yeah? "Nothing happened."

Andy smiled conspiratorially at him. "I know nothing happened, but tell me what happened."

"Why you raising this now?"

"Why not? She hasn't said anything, directly. But every now and again, she drops hints."

Andy could punch. "So what's her version?"

"I'm not interested in her version. What's yours?"

Andy could punch, hard. "I think she was a bit pissed one night," he tried to dismiss it.

"Is my woman, remember?" Andy actually laughed. "If she was gonna make a move, she'd just rip her clothes off."

"All right, she was a bit sober and just ripped her

clothes off. She got a bit rowdy when we went out to a party. I had to escort her home."

Andy gave an 'I can't be arsed about this' shrug and looked like he wasn't going to pursue the matter any further (*Phew!*), so he asked, "Aren't you going to ask me if *I* did anything?"

"No. I've known you a lot longer than I've known her, right. i KNOW you."

"We go back."

"Way back." Andy lent across and they touched fists.

Having suggested that he knew that something had gone down with Katrina whilst he was away, Andy was emphasising that there should be no secrets between them. But Steve didn't think he needed to know any more details about the Katrina incident.

All right then. "Is she criss or is she criss?"

"Oh yes, seriously criss!"

Andy rubbed his hands in expectation. "Horny?"

"You have to ask?"

"Well then? Details."

"Details like what?"

"Details like, was the other one there?" Andy lent over like he expected to hear news.

"Course not! She didn't even know about it until yesterday."

Andy looked gravely disappointed. "Oh. I thought you'd dealt with both."

"I have dealt with both."

"But why didn't you two's-up?"

Pervert! 'Marti, mind if Corrine joins us?' he had to laugh. "Look man, I'm good but I'm not that good."

"You didn't even try, did you?" Andy looked genuinely annoyed. "You see you, you're such a fucking wimp! I know you from time, man. Like that gal! Spit roast! She was bang up for it! What kind of bollocks did you chat, 'Naw, naw man, it just don't seem right'. What kind of fuckries was that? And now the same raas foolishness... And Denise, where does she fit in all this?"

"Denise?"

"Yeah."

"She doesn't."

Sitting back erect, animatedly Andy scratched the back of his head. "I could be wrong, but from the way they said it, it's Denise you got pregnant."

"What?!?!?!!!"

nineteen

She'd done crying. She wasn't going to shed another tear over this. Where was Corrine? She didn't know. As soon as they'd got in, without any explanation, Corrine went out. She wanted to, needed to, think about the future of her relationship with Corrine but thoughts of her mother kept interfering. Her mother had, on the day she'd tried to explain about her emerging feelings of homosexuality, instantly and irrevocably disowned her. "That isn't natural! Pure nastiness!" — the last words her mother had spoken to her. Until that day, she'd been the apple of her mum's eye.

Denise would never forget her mum's look of pride and the sense that all her sacrifices had been worth it on the day that she graduated with First Class honours. Jean, her younger sister by three years, was also there, already six months pregnant with the second child to the second father. Now, her mother had rejected her and reorientated her life around Jean and her four grandchildren. That rejection was total; as far as her mother was concerned, Denise might as well be dead.

It was nearly six years since, and only now when she had to speak to her again to tell her that, despite her sexuality, she was pregnant, that suppressed emotions were coming to the fore.

***

"What do you mean she doesn't want to talk to me?"

"I'm sure you can appreciate how Denise feels," she said in her most delicate tone then carefully added, "Steve, she needs time."

"But she doesn't want to talk to me till then?" he asked with a hint of bitterness.

"Denise doesn't feel up to speaking to you at the moment."

Andy put his hand on Steve's shoulder. Angrily Steve shook it off. "How long is this moment gonna last?" he asked with biting sarcasm.

This was starting to piss her off. And although she'd told herself to keep cool, she knew she had more than enough justification to retaliate. "Look," she tried giving him an ironic smile, "she isn't saying very much to me either. Come on, Steve, imagine how you'd feel!"

"She's got to talk to me."

"What would you want her to say to you?"

" 'Steve, I'm pregnant' would be a good place to start."

Although he wasn't shouting, she was fairly sure that Denise could hear him. "Well, you know she's pregnant. What else is there to say?"

"I know that I'm just the lodger, right, but if Andy hadn't come round when the fuck was somebody gonna get around to telling me?"

"You believe that Denise should speak to you. How about you having something to say to *me*?"

"Oh yeah." He turned back to face her. "Like what?"

"Like how you got my lover pregnant!"

Andy appeared to suddenly find the wallpaper fascinating, but Steve simply sneered down at her. "It's all my fault, yes? I have done something to her, right? She had nothing to do with it, I suppose?"

Bastard! "Don't avoid the issue. Andy, do me a favour, man. Pick her up and throw her out of the window for me will yah."

For a fleeting moment she thought he was being serious and that Andy might actually attempt to act on that request. The fact that she'd felt afraid, albeit for only an instant, made her even more annoyed and determined. Brushing past Andy, she walked up to Steve so that she was right 'in his face'. "Weren't you man enough to tell me to my face?"

Disdainfully looking over her head, he said, "Don't even bother opening it, Andy. Just straight out."

Moving even closer so that her breasts were almost touching his chest, she glared up at him. "You sat there gloating, didn't you? This was your way of getting back at the dyke who took your woman, wasn't it?"

"Fuck off Corrine!" he bellowed down at her. "I don't fucking believe this."

Smiling! The bastard was smiling. "Oh yes? What don't you believe?" He had made her girlfriend pregnant. She should be and wanted to be livid about that. But, she wasn't.

"Corrine, if you were a geezer, we could sort it, but you aren't."

"Our arrangement," Corrine started thoughtfully, was for me to get pregnant. From the start it was really her you wanted the baby with, wasn't it?"

"I know it's none of my business, but somebody is going to get hurt," Andy said seriously and stood up like he was going to put a stop to the bickering.

Andy had taken all this in like it was the best entertainment he'd had in years. "Remember primary school? Remember that idiot bwoy? The one where you're sitting there minding your own business and the damn fool would have to come and start bothering you. So you give him a slap. The next you know about it, him run gwan tell teacher that you hit him." Taking a slow deep breath he turned back to Steve, which is when Denise finally deigned to make an appearance.

He'd better watch it. Between the two of them they could land him back in hospital. Barely audibly he murmured, "Never trust anything that bleeds for five days and lives."

But Denise did hear him and, from the sound of it, she wasn't too happy about the comment.

"I want your backside out!" she yelled. "You get me? Who the fuck do you think you're talking to?"

twenty

Over the years he'd learned that whenever he got bad news, instead of getting too depressed about it, it was best to start looking around for good news. If he looked hard enough, he usually found some. That was exactly what he intended to do when Andy, who could be quite sensible when he wanted to be, casually asked, 'Do you remember Terry?'

Of course he remembered.

His platoon was down at RAF Odiham, playing with Chinook helicopters. There were also some Booties (Royal Marines) frollicking with the Chinooks. One evening, after 'a few' beers and a bit of banter, just to show these gobshite Comfort for the Navy how Bird Men did it, he climbed onto the roof of a two-story building and, with the lads egging him on, jumped off. Buoyed up by the pre-eminence of the Parachute Regiment, and because none of the brave Green Death would follow his example, he was bought 'a few' more beers.

The next morning they had a little jaunt — nothing really worth talking about, just a twelve-mile tab. P Company, Basic Fitness Tests, battle marches, march & shoots; for the first time ever, he couldn't keep up and got beasted. They took the gun away from him and beasted him some more. He still couldn't keep up. Turned out that he'd fucked his ankle and he was whisked off to spend a pleasant week, or so, at RAF Headley Court Hospital. This mollycoddling wasn't for his benefit, they wanted him fit to play football for the battalion.

He'd never looked at, let alone touched, a servicewoman. They were usually truffle hounds, lesbians or, if they were passably good-looking, they were also a long way up their own arse. It was the result of them being in a male dominated environment — they were just too used to men sniffing after them. He'd always thought that if a really ugly woman was seriously into cock, she should join the army. There, she'd find 'nuff men prepared to fuck anything with a hole in it.

The second time he did it, Andy, quite sensibly, asked why they were driving from Aldershot to Highbury via Headley Court. He wasn't even aware that he'd been doing it, so he explained: Terry — not Terri — was an Air Force nurse that he'd met. She was a year older, beautiful, approachable, funny, easy going, not up her own arse and a Flight Lieutenant. For a week, or so, they'd kinda 'clicked'.

That's when Andy stopped being sensible. 'Shag her?'

Lance Corporals didn't shag Flight Lieutenants. He never made a pass; never called her anything other than 'Ma'am'; never said or did anything inappropriate. And she really appreciated that. So, all they did was click — an intense, but unstated, 'if only' percolating between them. He wasn't in love with her nor was he infatuated with her but, unconsciously, he'd made wide detours on the off-chance of just seeing her. Of course, at the time, Andy thought this was piffle.

The point Andy, quite sensibly, was making by asking about Terry was whether Corrine, being a lesbian, was the Officer and he was still the Lance Corporal. Was he aware that he was in danger of making another wide detour on the off-chance of just seeing her?

The next day he got a taxi, went to work and walked straight into a massive bollocking from Naheed — he should be at home resting his knees! Things started looking up when a couple of the other mechanics came over and 'complained' about Naheed. She had a boyfriend! How did they know? She told them to 'Stop it!' when any of them tried flirting with her. She was being pretty damn firm about it, apparently. For obvious reasons he'd avoided thinking about this, but the fact remained that three guys at work had got into her knickers. It was slowly dawning on him that, sure, they got the sex but they hadn't got to the woman.

It was wholly in keeping with Naheed's role that she should 'organise' his getting home by offering him a lift that evening. This offer was not to be refused. At the end of the road, there was a choice: turn left for Fulham, right for Herne Hill. There wasn't a discussion, she turned right. Back at her flat, in an 'I'm still pissed off at you' sort of style, she fucked his brains out and then drove him home. Her parting shot was something along the lines of, 'If you're so stupid that you're going to come to work, then the least you could do is bring some clothes so that I don't have to drive all the way back to Fulham every night'.

***

"Hi Steve." Corrine was sitting on the bed next to him.

"Hi." Blinking sleep out of his eyes he started to sit up…

She lent over and gave him a smacker on the lips!

Her lips tasted of toothpaste. Toothpaste in the middle of the day? So she'd cleaned her teeth and walked in here with every intention of kissing him. Why was she doing this?

"Corrine, wouldn't Denise be pissed off if she saw you doing that?"

Instead of answering the question, she said, "Don't

worry, Steve, this is a dream. Sit up." And started helping him (as if he still needed help) to sit up. As soon as he had, she put her arms around him and kissed him some more. After a while she broke off and pulled back. "I know you can kiss better than that." Then she went back to her kissing, this time 'tongue and all'.

No. No. No. It didn't make sense. He wasn't having any of this. "Corrine, why are you kissing me?"

She gave him a business-like smile. "There are many reasons why I might want to kiss you. Can't you think of any?"

Off the top oh his head, he couldn't. "No, I can't."

Very serious, she stared into his eyes for a bit then said, "I'm sure you can." Then she kissed him again!

He took it and simply said, "I don't understand what I don't understand."

She swore she wasn't using him to get back at Denise. "OK then, let's get down to it."

"Look, Corrine, I'd make love to you at the drop of a hat but I can just feel it, Denise is gonna walk in here."

She gave him one of her 'Is there a problem here?' looks then said, "So you would like to?"

"Would I like to make love to you? Yes. Would I like to do it right now? No. Why? Denise, that's why. Anyway, last time you said that that would be the last time."

She put her arms around him, pulled him in tight and planted a dynamite kiss on his lips! Reluctantly he pulled away.

"But Denise…"

She wasn't having any of that and started climbing on him. "You like my breasts, don't you? Undo my bra."

Whipping off her bins, then crossing her arms, she pulled her rugby shirt off over her head and slipped off her bra.

"Corrine! Excuse me. But what are you doing?"

"I want you to remember me," she said like that explained everything.

"I don't care what you say. If Denise was to walk in here… I'm in enough shit as it is. OK."

Now she was fucking about with her belt. "I'll always remember you." It was like she was had a totally different agenda and ignoring anything that he said. "And I want you to remember me." Standing up she pulled down her jeans, stepped out of them and paraded half naked before him. By the time she'd wiggled out of her knickers, she seemed to have chilled, a bit.

"Will you remember me, Steve?"

"Yes. No, I'm not just saying that. Now Corrine, if you want to make me really happy, just put your clothes on before she comes in here."

Did she? *Did she fuck!* Throwing an arm around his neck, she plonked herself across his thighs, away from his knees and, arching her back, stuck her tits in his face. "I will always remember you, do you understand?"

"Yeah, yeah, yeah. Now get off me."

"I mean it, Steve. Remember me, it's important. OK?"

"Even if I wanted to, I don't think I could ever forget you."

Finally, the woman seemed to accept this. Giving him one more kiss, she eased herself off the bed. She seemed content, gave him one more 'look' then turned and left.

Laying back and staring at the ceiling, it occurred to him that he'd better start flat hunting soon. Or get his own flat back. He sighed, hoping that one day he was going to look back at all this and laugh. He hoped that that day wouldn't be too far in the future.

twenty-one

In the end she was left no option but to summarily deliver to Steve, Denise's 'never darken our doorstep' chat: 'Move out within one week. After that, you'll make no contact, directly or indirectly, with either Denise or me. You will have no responsibilities or ties to our child — it will not be given your surname. You will not, in any circumstances or at any time, attempt to see, meet, make overtures, get to know, or make yourself known to, the aforementioned child. Now fuck off and have a nice life!'

Compelled to prising a response out of him, she asked what was he going to do.

'I've found somewhere. I'll leave now', was his answer. Then sullenly, he got up, pulled out his rucksack and started packing.

"Do one thing for me, please. If it's a boy, make sure he supports Arsenal. OK?"

"I'm a Chelsea fan," was Denise's instantaneous rebuttal.

Bitch! Denise didn't know anything about football. Bitch! Bitch! Bitch!

With that same imperceptible raising of his eyebrow, that same 'you can't hurt me' expression, he continued down the stairs. Without a backward glance he opened the front door and stepped out.

As the door closed, Corrine whispered, "I'm also pregnant Steve.

epilogue

It's three all and it's their corner. This is probably the last kick of the match; players are swarming all over the penalty area. Everybody, including their goalie, has come up for this. The ball is hit deep past the far post. He finds himself rising high above the defenders to meet it. He makes contact with the ball but is falling backwards because while airborne someone has smacked into his legs. He hears the jubilant shouts as he hits the deck, then the whistle for the goal immediately followed by the one for full time. His team mates are piling on top of him. He's scored the winner!

It's not just that they've won a Cup tie. Nor because he is the hero of the day. But because he got himself fit, made it back to the first team and played a full ninety minutes. What do those doctors know? It was all down to the sports injury specialist, physiotherapy and hard work — against all the odds he'd made it.

The team is going for a beer or two or several. Andy can't believe he isn't going with them. Jumping into his gleaming blood red, drop top, Triumph Stag, he doesn't put on the stereo. All the way there he listens to the supercharged engine, above the steady whistle of the wind, as it purrs; that's exactly how he feels, purring. When he pulls up, he doesn't open the door but leaps out of the Stag. He feels as agile as a cat and takes the stairs two at a time. Accelerating as if going for the header, he launches himself — a flying kick and the door crashes open. He lands gracefully and strolls in.

A short white guy flies out of the bedroom and squares up to him in the hall. But the guy must have seen something in his face because he doesn't make a move. Just as well, because the mood he is in just then, he'd take on the heavyweight champion of the world, and win. Pulling on a dressing gown, Tracy comes out behind the guy. He keeps his attention on the guy. "You know who I am. Leave."

The guy hesitates but is smart enough to recognise that not only is he facing someone who who will not be messed with. The guy drifts back into the room and comes out with his shirt and coat. Looking at Tracy then at him, the guy seems to be shaping up to try and defend her. Keeping his eyes on shortarse he says, "Wait for her outside." The guy turns to check with her, then brushes past him and goes out.

She stomps back into the room and he cruises in after her. She looks ready to hand out another of her tongue lashings. "Park your arse," he pre-empts her. Slightly fearful, she sits on the bed. "Pack. Leave with just what you came with." She can see that there is no arguing with him but she still has to have a dig, "Well, get out and let me get dressed." Backing out of the room, he props himself against a wall in the corridor and patiently waits while she takes her time packing. Four suitcases full. He helps her carry them down the steps then shortarse takes over. There is only one more thing he has to say to her, "Tracy, I'm sorry I hit you." She doesn't answer.

Watching them load the car and drive off, he doesn't feel particularly elated — just tidying up a loose end. Walking back into the flat, he examines the doorframe. Not much damage; nothing he couldn't fix in a couple of hours. First things first. He phones Naheed, gives her the address and asks her to come over. Surprisingly, she doesn't ask what's the urgency, she simply says she'll see him in a little while. Going to the cupboard, he pulls out his tool box. Tracy had been in it; only a woman would mix ring spanners with open spanners.

During his fixing of the doorframe Naheed arrives all tarted up in a mini dress with a see-through V neck that barely managed to hide her tits. The dress was so short that even with her facing him, he could tell that it exposed the bottom half of her arse. Hmm... Must be wearing a thong.

Giving him a friendly kiss from those luscious red lips she said, "So what can I get you?"

"What?"

"It's lunch time, have you eaten?"

All he could utter was an incredulous, "No."

"So what would you like?" The look she gives him implies 'there's dew in the valleys — somewhere something is moist'.

Sitting her down in the living room and slipping in next to her, he starts: "This is my flat, I mean I live here but it isn't my home. Do you understand?"

Looking intently at him, she shakes her head.

"I mean, I would think of it as my home if you were here with me."

Eyes becoming slightly watery, she takes his hand, "Steve, I love you, I really do, but I don't know."

"And I love you, I can't think of anything that would make me happier. I want you in my life, always."

"Are you asking me to marry you?" A single tear flows down her left cheek.

"Yes."

She doesn't say anything but continues to look at him anxiously. Why doesn't she answer? Because he hasn't asked. Sliding down on one knee he says, "Naheed, will you marry me?"

Instead of answering, she tearfully stares at his hand, gives him a half painful, half amused smile, then says, "My mother said to only marry a man who has clean fingernails and collar." Then burying her head in his shoulder, she starts to cry. "Steve, you hardly know anything about me."

Not the response he was expecting. "True, but I know I love you with all my heart."

She bawls some more into his shoulder. He's lost the plot. She's crying like he'd just told her he was kicking her into touch. "Naheed, I don't know how to explain just how much I love you."

He could feel her trembling as she asks, "Do you love me unconditionally?"

Unconditionally? That means warts and all, doesn't it? That goes without saying. "Yes, unconditionally."

Taking her head off his shoulder, weepily, timidly, almost fearfully, she stares into his eyes. "Even if I'm bisexual?"

END